Snatched Up by a Don 3

A BBW LOVE STORY

P. WISE

Contents

Stay Connected!

Website: PrettiWise.com
Instagram: @CEO.Pwise
Facebook: Author P. Wise
Facebook Business: Authoress P. Wise
Facebook Group: Words of the Wise (P. Wise Book Group)

PREVIOUSLY

LOGAN

It had been a couple of days since the whole ordeal with Cat and Lyric. I hadn't spoken to or saw Cat at all, and I didn't frequent downstairs as much either. Although I spoke my truth to Lyric, I had to do the same with Cat to actually feel right about everything. So, until I told Cat what it was, I kept my distance from Lyric, even though it pained me to do so.

The days had been quiet. My father hadn't hit me up to handle anything, and there wasn't shit going on in the house. I just used it as time to kick back and sort things out in my head. One thing I couldn't complain about was having some peace and quiet.

While watching the New York Knicks play the Boston Celtics, my phone started to ring. I was a little annoyed because it was the last few seconds of the game, and it was tied. Looking at the screen, my Pops' name appeared.

"Wassup, Pa," I answered.

"What's up, kid? What you up to?" he asked.

"Shit, just watching a game; what you need?"

"Dinner tonight at my place. De León will be in attendance," he informed me.

Oh, fuck no, I thought.

"How long was this planned?" I asked.

"Not long, just make sure and be here. I gotta go." He hung up.

While I still needed to holla at Cat, I didn't expect her father to be coming into town. If I ended up leaving her, which was my plan, I wasn't sure how things would end up between our families. I was hoping he understood and didn't make a big deal of it. The only way he would probably be somewhat okay with it was if Cat agreed to the split, which she should've wanted. We both weren't happy.

As soon as I rested my phone down, it chimed. Someone had set the motion detector off at the gate. When I went to the camera, I saw it was Cat driving in. Automatically, I thought, *what a coincidence.*

I leaned back on the couch and didn't even move. She was probably still upset and didn't want to see me. The only reason she was back home was most likely because her father was coming and she wanted to put on a fake front for him.

It was still a bit early in the day, so we had a lot of time to get ready for the night. I flipped the channel and landed on another game that was just starting. Kicking up my feet, I relaxed and tuned into the Sixers against the Wolves. Not trying to leave out my man cave, I stayed put for hours until it was time for me to get ready for dinner.

I dreaded the moment I had to come face to face with Cat, but it was inevitable. I went upstairs to our bedroom and found her rubbing lotion on her legs on the loveseat. When I walked in, she looked up at me for a quick second and returned her gaze to her legs. Her body language was giving unbothered, so I continued on my way to the walk-in closet.

Picking out a calm fit for the night, I laid it out on the bed and plugged my phone up to the charger before hopping in the shower. Handling my cleanliness and everything associated with it, I got out the bathroom to get dressed. Cat wasn't in the room, but her scent of perfume lingered in the air strongly.

I looked at the time on my phone and saw I had to pick up my pace just a little bit. I slipped into my Amiri jeans and t-shirt, stepped into my Dior's, and tied my laces. Brushing my hair to level out my waves, I put on my jewelry to complement my look.

Now, that's a fly ass nigga, I thought as I looked myself up and down in the mirror.

Grabbing my phone off the charger, I checked the camera to see what Lyric was up to. When I clicked on her surveillance, I saw she was chilling, writing in her book. Closing the app, I picked up my wallet and a wad of cash from my nightstand, headed downstairs to see where Cat was.

"Cat!" I yelled as I descended the stairs.

"What?" she answered.

"You ready?" I asked.

She didn't respond; instead, she came walking out from the living room area looking fine as hell. Cat was undeniably beautiful, but looks wasn't always it for me; I needed more.

"What it look like?" She rolled her eyes.

If going in separate cars was on the table, we would've done that. Since our parents didn't know what was going on, we had to keep things under wraps until we knew exactly what we were doing and how we were going to do it.

"Come on, man," I grilled as I went to open the front door.

She walked out before me, and I followed. I hit the unlock button on my Porsche and watched her get in as normal. When I got in, I felt tension all through the car and the feeling was just bad. I turned on the music, raising the volume as I pulled off the property.

Most of the ride to my father's house, we didn't say a word to one another. Coming close to arriving, she lowered the music and decided she wanted to speak.

"Why don't you love me?" she blurted out.

Sighing heavily, I took a quick look at her and returned my attention back on the road. "I love you, Cat. What you talking about?"

"So, why you fucked that bitch for?" she spat.

I pinched the bridge of my nose with my free hand. "Cat, I'm about to be so real with you right now; I just hope you can take it."

"Go ahead Logan; it's what I've been waiting for."

"I love you, I do, but I'm in love with someone else and I can't keep lying to you or myself about it," I confessed.

She leaned back in her seat and looked forward. Not a word came out of her mouth, she just stayed quiet. While I was expecting her to start bugging out and cursing up a storm, she continued to sit there and stare at the road ahead of us.

The rest of the ride was like the beginning, quiet between the two of us and the only thing that was heard was the music playing.

Not long after, we arrived at my Pop's spot. Pulling in, I saw there were extra cars parked on the property, which let me know Cat's father was already in attendance. We got out the car and made our way up the front steps. The door was opened by the maid before we even had to knock or ring the doorbell. As soon as we entered, both of our fathers were walking towards us from the direction of the office. It looked like they had already settled business, which was a good thing. I didn't have to spend any extra time here once dinner was over.

"Princesa!" De León exclaimed when he laid eyes on Cat.

"Hola, Papi." She made her way into his embrace.

I watched the two greet each other while I went around them and hollered at my Pops. "Everything good?" I asked as I dapped him up.

"Everything's great." He smiled.

"Logan, what's the deal my son-in-law?" De León turned around and asked.

"Same ol', same ol'. You good?" I asked, as we gave each other a firm hug.

"Sí, I cannot complain," he said in his thick Spanish accent.

"Good, good."

"Let us eat," my father announced.

Yes, let us so I can get the fuck up outta here, I thought.

We all walked off and went into the dining room. Taking our appropriate seats around the table, my father nodded and made sure I sat across from him at the other head of the table. I'd usually sit next to him, so it took me aback and I wondered what that was all about. I knew not to question him in front of company, so I left it at the back of my mind for a later time.

The food came out and everyone dug in. Looking over at my father and De León, they were so into eating and discussing some business ideas, they didn't even notice the tension between Cat and me. Although we tried our best to keep it normal, it was hard after having that brief conversation in the car right before getting to the dinner.

"Excuse me." Cat dropped the fork out of nowhere before standing up abruptly.

She stormed out the dining room and went to what I assumed the restroom. While I wanted to go after her as a husband should've, I decided to give her a minute before seeing what the hell was wrong. It wasn't like I was even speaking to make her irritated or anything.

"Is she okay?" her father asked out of concern.

"Yeah, I'll go check on her in a second," I told him.

The two returned to their conversation as if nothing happened. Meanwhile, I had an urge to see Lyric. I wanted to know what she was doing, what she was thinking, if she needed anything. Checking the surveillance on my phone, I saw she was doing the same thing just like when I left, writing.

As I was closing out the app on my phone, my father stood and excused himself from the table as well. He went in the same direction Cat did, so I also assumed he went to either the restroom or his office since both were in that direction.

"So, Logan, what have you been up to?" De León asked.

"Just the regular, following all the old man's orders," I joked, making us both chuckle.

"I know how that can be, I was the same way with my papa when I was younger. Now, my son is getting older and about to be just like you."

"Well, at least he have you and don't have a father like me," I cracked.

"You're so funny amigo."

We laughed and made a quick toast to sons following in their fathers' footsteps.

"Let me go and check on her. I'll be right back," I told him.

He nodded and continued eating his dessert.

Walking towards the bathroom, the closer I got, I heard people speaking in hushed tones. Every step I took though, it started to become clearer and clearer; it was my father and Cat talking. I kept my distance where I was still able to hear what it was they were going back and forth about.

"Don't touch me," Cat snapped.

"Now you want to act like that. Keep playing with me and you'll see how I can turn your world upside down," my father told her.

"It's already upside down so, at this point, I don't give a fuck. Leave me alone, you sick fuck."

Wap!

I heard him slap her, which made me want to intervene but I wasn't finished eavesdropping just yet. I knew more was about to come.

"You seriously going to just slap me while my father is sitting a few feet away?"

"Bitch, I own you. I don't give a fuck about your father. I should make you suck my dick right here, right now."

"Please don't do this. I told you we have to end things. I need to make things right with your son before he leaves me," she cried.

On that note, I felt it was time I entered the party. "Consider yourself left, bitch," I stepped around the corner and spat.

"Logan!" She covered her mouth.

My father stood there in complete shock and didn't know what to do next. Shit, I didn't know what to do. All sorts of mixed emotions took over me. I wasn't sure if to just walk away or put a bullet in both their heads. The menace in me decided to pull my gun out from my back and point it at them.

"You have lost your fuckin' mind," my father fumed.

"Nah, you did when you started fuckin' my wife. What type of timing you on man?"

"Logan, please, just put the gun down," she cried out loud.

I heard footsteps rushing towards me; that's when I knew her loud ass had alerted my Pops' men or even her father's.

Without turning around, I knew they were behind me with

their weapons drawn. My father used his hands to signal to them to not shoot, but I didn't care. If I had decided to pull the trigger, I would've went out guns blazing.

"What is going on here?" I heard De León approaching us. He stood beside me with a confused look on his face.

"Tell him, Cat, what's going on?" I scolded.

She just continued to cry and didn't want to make eye contact with any one of us.

"Your daughter been fuckin' my father," I blurted out.

"What?" he shouted.

Immediately, he started talking some shit in Spanish and, while some I understood, the rest he could've missed me with the shit.

"How long, Catteleya?" he asked her.

"Yeah, how long?" I added.

She didn't answer; she just kept on crying.

"Logan, please lower your gun," De León begged.

"No."

"If you don't, I will take it as a sign of disrespect and I won't have a choice but—"

"What the fuck you gon' do?" I turned to him and asked.

His nose flared up and he became a bit pink. Bosses always had a problem when someone else stood up to them; their first thought was to always kill or hurt. I didn't give a fuck about neither one of their titles, position, or power. I was a man and my pride meant everything to me.

"You know what, fuck y'all, fuck this," I gritted.

I placed my gun back in my waistband, turned around and

pushed pass all the men that were behind me. Not one of them did anything, they knew better.

Rushing out of the house, I jumped in my car, quickly started it up and drove off the estate. I couldn't help but feel defeated and betrayed. Out of all the things in the world to happen to me, the people I loved fucked me over.

Joe was at the house making sure everything was straight there. I got on my phone and rang him.

"Yeah, Lo," he answered on the first ring.

"Go in both the safes, pack everything into two duffle bags. Make sure my important documents are in there," I instructed him.

"I'm on it." He hung up.

Pressing on nothing but gas, I weaved in and out of traffic, trying to make my way home. Cutting my travel time in damn near half, I was pulling into my spot. Joe was already at the door with both bags.

"Where you want me to put this?" he asked.

"You can put it in the Porsche," I told him.

While he went and loaded the car up, I ran downstairs to Lyric. "Open this shit now!" I yelled as I walked up to the door.

When it was open, Lyric looked startled; she must've heard the bass in my voice.

"Grab your books and shit. I'm leaving and I'm taking you with me," I told him.

She stood stagnant for a minute with a confused look. I sensed some kind of hesitation but, after a moment or two, she snapped out of whatever it was she was thinking and started gathering up her stuff.

"Just get your books and shit. Everything else, don't worry about it. I'll get you all new shit."

"Okay, okay." She grabbed her books, slipped her feet in the bedroom slippers I bought her, and was ready to dip.

I grabbed her hand, as we ran out the room and up the stairs. Joe was standing outside the car waiting for me to come out.

"Get the emergency burner and wait for my call," I told him as I got Lyric inside the front seat of the car.

"I'll be waiting," he said.

I jumped in the driver seat and put the car in drive. Speeding out from my roundabout driveway, I was pulling out the gate and onto the street when we were smacked by an SUV, making the Porsche flip over three times.

CHAPTER 1

LOGAN

One month later...

"You pussies really think I came this far to let y'all hit me out? I'm slidin' through the trenches, bulletproof car, they can't even take me out," Meek Mill rapped on his freestyle, *God Did*.

I was on my third set of bench presses and a whole hour into my workout. My body was hot and sweaty, arms were burning, but it was all stimulating my mind and kept me busy and distracted. The past few weeks, I couldn't really do anything but focus on Lyric, work out, and make sure we weren't found.

"You ready to go for your run?" Joe came into the workout room and asked.

"Yeah, let's go." I placed the bar on the hook and got up. "She's good?" I turned and asked him.

"She's fine, Lo," he assured me.

I took a gulp of my water bottle, wiped my face of sweat, and headed out the door. As I reached outside, the spring fresh air brushed my face. I stretched out my legs and got prepared for my run, as Joe hoped in the SUV.

Looking back at the beach house we were occupying, I scanned the premises to make sure all the guys were positioned where they needed to be. Satisfied with the scene, I turned around, placed my Air Pods in my ears, and started to lightly jog away from the house as Joe drove close behind me.

The faster my feet ran, the quicker I sunk into my head. No matter how many days had past, I thought about what happened that day I found out my wife was fucking my father. I didn't only think about the revelation but also about how Lyric and my life was almost taken.

Lucky for us, Joe was on point and got the rest of the guys that was at the house to come out and light up the men my Pops sent for us. While my Porsche was flipped multiple times, we survived. I had some bruises and a graze from one of the guys shooting at me, but it wasn't nothing major. Overall, I was great but, Lyric, she wasn't.

Lyric banged her head so hard during the accident, she was knocked unconscious immediately. When we got a doctor to her, he informed us she was in a coma and would come out when she was ready. Besides being in a deep sleep, Lyric suffered a broken hand, the one she wrote with.

From the moment shit went down, I'd been feeling so fucked up and at fault. If I had left her there, she wouldn't had been in the predicament she was in. I blamed myself day in and day out every time I sat by her bed side praying she woke up.

Beep! Beep! Beep!

I heard the sound of a vehicle horn coming through my Air Pods. I turned and saw Joe waving at me, so I slowed down for him to drive up next to me.

"What's good?" I asked.

"You got enough in?" he quizzed.

"Yeah but, I mean, I can go a little more. Why wassup?"

"The doctor at the house to check on Lyric," he informed me.

"Shit, that's today?"

I totally forgot he was coming to see about her hand. He was supposed to be taking off the cast to examine her hand.

"Yeah, so come on."

I turned around and started running back in the direction of the house. By the time we reached back, the doctor was already conducting his checkup. He was cutting through the cast when I walked in.

"Mr. Luchiano, hello," the older black man greeted.

"Wassup, doc. How's it looking?" I asked, taking a step closer.

"Let's see." He continued to remove the cast.

Moments later, he cleaned off any remains and massaged her hand to feel where it was broken. Turning around with a smile on his face, he nodded his head up and down, then gave me a thumbs up.

"Looks and feels good. She will have to do some therapy once she wakes in order to use her hands like she once did before," he advised.

"Understandable. I hope that'll be soon," I voiced.

He turned and looked at her vitals that were on the screen next to her bed. "Hopefully," he added.

"Yeah, I miss her," I said above a whisper.

I left the room and allowed him his space to finish his thorough check up on her. My ass started feeling crazy from all the sweat anyway, so I went and jumped in the shower. The second I started to apply soap to my skin, I heard someone knocking on the bathroom door. It was only one person who was able to get inside my room without any problems, so it had to be Joe.

"Yo!" I yelled from inside the shower.

"Logan, get out, now. It's Lyric!" Joe yelled from behind the door.

His voice was filled with excitement, so I knew it had to be good news, or at least I prayed it was. I quickly rinsed the studs that covered my body, turned off the water, and got out the shower. Drying my skin as fast as possible, I went into my room and threw on some sweats with no draws, then ran out the door. Joe was standing right outside waiting for me. Following his lead, we entered the room where Lyric was being taken care of.

The moment I stepped foot inside and saw Lyric awake and

functioning, I felt tears welling up in my eyes. I was stuck at the entrance of the room as if my feet were cemented to the ground. Although I wanted her to wake up, I just couldn't believe my eyes. It was like she heard me a little earlier when I said I missed her, or maybe it was the doctor removing her cast. Knowing Lyric, she probably felt that and knew it was time to get up and write.

We stared at each other for a minute. The room stood still while everyone around us just looked on. Slowly moving in her direction, I forced one foot in front the other until I was finally standing in front of her.

"Baby girl, I-I—"

"Shhh." She placed her finger on her lips and used the other index finger to call me closer to her.

I sat at the edge of the bed, reached down, and pulled her into my arms. With the little strength she had, she held onto me tightly like she didn't want me to go anywhere.

"I'm sorry," I whispered.

"Don't be," she told me, followed by a hard cough.

"She has to drink lots of fluids," the doctor intervened and said.

He brought her over a bottle of water, and she took it with her left hand. In one drink, she finished the entire sixteen-ounce bottle.

"Thirsty ass," I joked.

She cracked a smile and giggled like a school girl.

There she goes, I thought.

"I know you two want to spend time, so let me hurry and

run my tests, that way I can get out of you all way," the doctor alerted us.

"Yeah, go ahead doc," I told him.

I kissed her lips gently before standing up. The doctor went right to work on her, checking everything, down to drawing blood. While he was tending to Lyric, I used the time to go back and finish handling my hygiene. By the time I was finished and went to check on them, he was wrapping up.

"I'll call you in a few hours with the test results," he said before exiting out the room.

Once he disappeared, I made my way back over to Lyric, who was sitting right up in the bed rotating her wrist.

"How you feeling?" I asked as I took a seat at the edge.

"Alive." She smiled. "I'm good. I just want to take a good shower, get some food in my stomach, and just relax."

"We can definitely make that happen." I grabbed ahold of her hand. "Charisse!" I yelled out to the in-house nurse.

From the moment we got settled into the beach house and the doctor came by, he recommend having a nurse around for her, so I did just that. Charisse helped with not only Lyric's medical things, but she made sure her hygiene was taken care of.

Of course I wanted to spend time with her but I knew, just waking up, she wanted to adjust and get herself together.

"Yes Sir." Charisse walked into the room.

"She wants to get in the bath and all that good shit, take care of her for me," I directed. She nodded her head while smiling.

I gave Lyric a kiss on her weak hand and made my way out

the room, once again. Joe cornered me, as I was making my way downstairs to the kitchen to prepare something for Lyric to eat.

"I'm glad she's okay," he stated.

I turned and looked at him as I opened the fridge door. "Yeah, thanks to you she is. Thanks again for saving our lives, man; I owe you."

"Logan, seriously? I was only doing my job, the job I had since we were younger," he tried to water down the compliment.

"Call it what you want, you're a real one my G." I dapped him up.

Joe had been around since my teenage days; he was a little older than I was but not by far. He was a full-blown Italian but, being around me for years, he got hipped to that New York shit. I never called anyone my friend ever since I left my real friends from my old hood behind, but Joe was definitely the closest thing I had to a friend; he was more so family.

"What you about to make her to eat? You know your ass can't cook, man," he cracked.

"Fuck you, nigga." I waved him off.

The house was stocked up like crazy with all types of shit to eat, snack on, and drink. I even had some liquor on deck; there were some nights I needed to feel a little nice dealing with all the stress.

"The chef should be here any minute to prepare dinner, just fix her a sandwich in the meantime," he suggested.

"Yeah, you right. I'll even make her a nice lil' drink," I agreed.

Joe chuckled and left the kitchen, leaving me to pretend I was some kind of cook and knew what I was doing.

About an hour later, Charisse came and found me in the living room watching TV.

"She's finished, Sir," she informed me.

"Good lookin', Charisse."

As fast as she came, she left. I jumped off the couch and went into the kitchen to grab the sandwich I made her not long before, along with the drink and a bottle of water.

When I got to her room, Lyric was standing by the window looking out at the ocean. It was a beautiful view, so I made sure she was set up in that room.

"Nice as shit, ain't it?" I asked her.

She turned around and beamed brightly when she saw me standing there. My heart skipped a couple beats once I saw how much she was glowing and seemly in a good place despite our predicament.

"Hell yeah it is; wish we can stay here forever." She hung her head.

I cleared my throat and stepped closer. "I made you a sandwich and a drink. The Chef is cooking dinner now." I placed the plate, glass, and bottled water I had under my arm onto the table that was in the room.

"Thanks, baby," she said sweetly.

My phone started to ring, interrupting our moment. Just when I was about to ignore whoever it was, I changed my mind once I saw it was the doctor. "Yeah, doc," I answered the phone.

"Logan, I got her lab results back," he stated. "Everything

looks great, no problems at all. We just have to focus on doing therapy for her hand."

"Nice, that's great news."

I raised my thumb up at Lyric, signaling that everything was fine. She had sat down at the table and was about to start munching on her sandwich.

"There's one thing though," he paused.

"What is it?" I asked in a concerned tone.

"Lyric's pregnant."

She's what? I yelled in my own head.

"You sure?" I asked as I looked at her taking a bite of her meal.

"A hundred percent positive. We need to get her an ultrasound and run tests pertaining to that," he advised.

Lyric picked up the glass that contained the alcoholic drink I made for her. Without wasting a second, I leaped over to her and snatched the glass from her hand. She looked at me like I had five heads, but I ignored her for the time being.

"Okay, so come by when you can and handle all of that," I told him.

"I'll be by tomorrow."

"Thanks, doc." I hung up.

"Give me back my drink; what's wrong with you?" she asked, scrunching up her face.

"Lyric, you can't drink this shit, man."

"Why not? I was asleep for a month and been through hell, I need a—"

"You're pregnant," I blurted out.

CHAPTER 2

LYRIC

"Pregnant? Yeah, right, that has to be a mistake," I laughed.

Logan stood there with the most serious face on and never moved an inched.

"Wait, you're serious," I changed my tone.

"Very, the doctor just told me. He got all your test results back and that's how he found out," he informed me.

"But, how?" I asked out loud and to no one in particular.

Chadd and I had been trying for so long and, since we had no luck, I went and got check and found out I had PCOS. The doctor told me I would've had a difficult time conceiving with that diagnosis. But as soon as Logan shoots the club up, I'm pregnant?

I guess God had his plans, I thought to myself.

Being so caught up in my head, I didn't notice Logan had taken a seat at the foot of the bed. He was staring at the wall in a complete zone. I could've only imagined what was running through his mind. We were on the run, both still married, and now starting to build a relationship between the two of us.

"Logan," I spoke softly.

He quickly snapped out of his trance and looked at me. "Yeah," he answered.

I took a seat next to him. "You okay? I know it's a lot. If you don't want—"

"Don't want what, Lyric?" he turned and spat.

"I was only saying—"

"Don't say anything Lyric because I know for a fact you ain't about to have anything dealing with an abortion or adoption come out of your mouth," he stated in a serious tone.

I hung my head because that's exactly what I was thinking. Growing up, I was always the type of person who would make a decision to better a situation, even if it meant hurting myself. Our situation was very difficult, so I was willing to take the burden off his back or anyone else's and deal with it myself, even if it meant me taking the baby and raising it alone.

It got quiet as silence filled the room; the only thing that was heard were the waves crashing against the shore.

"Want to take a walk on the beach?" I spoke up and asked.

"Yeah, come on, a nigga need some air," he agreed.

He took my hand, led me out the room and through the house. We exited out the back where I saw a few men walking around. It was my first time seeing the place inside and out, but I kind of figured Logan would've had a ton of security knowing the threat that was lurking.

Although Logan didn't tell me what exactly happened, I placed two and two together and figured it out, or at least I did somewhat. The way he came in and grabbed me up from the basement and the accident wasn't no coincidence. Someone was after us, and I could've bet my last dollar that it was his father, along with Cat close behind.

We slipped off our slides and walked onto the sand, allowing our feet to sink into the cool, soft grainy feeling. The sun was almost completely gone, and the night sky was slowly taking over. My body felt a little weak but I held onto Logan, as we continued to the water.

"What's on your mind?" I broke the silence.

"A whole lot of shit," he chuckled.

"I know the feeling. I honestly don't know how to feel," I confessed.

"What you mean?" he asked.

"I always envision me learning that I'm with child to be a joyful moment. While I'm happy about the news because I didn't know it was possible, I can't help but feel sad about it too."

"Why sad?"

"You don't seem to be in a good light about the news, and look at our predicament. You still haven't told me what the hell is going on. I just know some shit is up," I voiced.

Logan stopped walking and stood in front of me. He

motioned for us to take a seat, so we both plopped down onto the sand, facing the water.

"Listen, Lyric, don't get me wrong, I'm ecstatic about the baby. If I didn't want it, I would've allowed you to drink that drink I made you. It just was a big shock, something I didn't expect at all, well, at least not right now. But, trust and believe, I got us, you don't ever have to doubt that, you hear me?"

I nodded my head as tears welled up in my eyes. He grabbed the side of my face with his hand, leaned in, and kissed me deeply.

"I love you," I backed away and said.

"I love you, baby girl."

We stayed by the shore for another hour, just talking and enjoying the view. Joe called Logan to tell him dinner was ready, so we got up and went back inside to eat, something I was dying to do; those IVs weren't it for me.

AFTER DINNER, WE CUDDLED UP AND WATCHED A movie together. It was a different feel since we hadn't done it in a while. We used to have moments like that right before his father ordered my kidnapping. Not trying to think about the past, I just enjoyed the present and prayed that it would be a future.

Logan filled me in on what transpired between his father and him. He informed me about the betrayal he experienced with Cat and was very honest and open about his feelings. I never thought I would've been able to get him to be up front with me like he was. A man of his statue was the type to keep things to himself and not show emotion, but he let it all out with me, and I appreciated that.

"I'm feening for some ice cream," he blurted out in the middle of the movie.

"That was mad random," I giggled.

"I know, it just came over me. You want some?"

"Yeah." I smiled.

He jumped out the bed and left the room. Ice cream didn't sound too bad to me. Dinner was great, so it was going to be the perfect dessert. I started back feeling like myself despite my hand being a little weak but, overall, I regained some strength.

Not long after, Logan returned with a big bucket of cookies and cream ice cream and two spoons in his hands. He hopped back into bed and handed me a spoon. Tapping my spoon with his as if it was a toast, he dug right in like a little kid. Once we had that talk out on the beach, his mood lightened up and he became the Logan I knew.

"Damn, you acting like you didn't just eat dinner," I teased.

Scoop after scoop, he was digging in the bucket.

"Don't worry about me. Mind your business and eat before it won't be no more," he chuckled.

Logan took a large scoop and forced it in my mouth, making some fall onto my chest. Instead of taking the tissue that was on the nightstand and cleaning it up, he used his mouth to slurp it up.

While all the ice cream was gone, he continued to slick and

suck around my breast, eventually pulling it out of the dress and bra. The bucket of ice cream and spoons were now on the floor, and Logan was on his quest to please not only himself but me.

When one piece of my clothing dropped, a piece of his did as well. Never did he stop kissing and caressing my body all over. Every single time his soft lips touched my skin, I felt butterflies flutter more and more in my stomach.

Kissing me gently but passionately, Logan found his hand between my legs and toyed with my lady part. I knew she was swollen and, just a little while after, I felt a flow of warmth coming out of me. He inserted a finger and then another, moving them in and out of me as I moved my hips in a circle to get a better feel.

I was over with the games and wanted him inside me. Pulling his hand away from me, I reached down to his dick with my strong hand and placed it at my opening. The look on his face was priceless but, once he got the hint, he did what he was supposed to, ram his way inside of me.

"Ughhh," I moaned out loud.

Feeling his head touching my cervix sent me straight into a frenzy. Logan filled me up like he usually did and worked his way in, out and all around. He knew how to move his hips and catch every angle of my honey pot. Logan wasn't one of those guys that just stuck his dick in you and penetrated in and out; he knew how to work his tool to make sure you felt all of it.

He hiked my legs up as far as they could've went, which was further than before. I lost some weight while I was in the coma, so I was feeling a bit more flexible than I did before and sexy at that. When he got a good rhythm, he reached for my neck and gave it a good enough squeeze as he drilled in and out of me.

Grabbing onto his waist, I dug my nails into his side and back as I took the painful pleasure he was delivering.

"Damn, ya pussy feel mad good," he groaned in a husky tone.

"You feel good, baby," I cooed.

He pulled out and tapped my side, motioning for me to turn around. When I was on all fours, making sure to rest on my forearms, he gave my right ass cheek a nice slap. Without warning, he forcefully entered me from behind.

"Shiiittt!" I yelped out loud.

"Shut up and take this dick," he said in a sexy ass voice.

"Okayyy, baby…" I whined.

And that's exactly what I did. I arched my back, as he grabbed my waist and gave me all the deep fast strokes. Logan wasn't showing me any mercy, but I sure didn't mind nor complained.

I felt myself about to cum again when he leaned over and started to plant kisses all over my back. He pushed my upper body down onto the bed, with my ass stuck in the air as he sped up. By the way he was moving and the feel of his dick, I knew he was near and so was I.

Moments later, I creamed all over his dick. He exploded and dumped all of his cum deep inside of me. Out of breath, we both laid back on the bed breathing heavily.

"Well, at least we know one is baking in there, so no more can come from that," I cracked.

We both bussed out laughing. He grabbed my face, making me turn towards him as he pecked my lips.

"I love you, Lyric."

"I love you more, Logan."

We cuddled up and fell right to sleep in each other's arms, a place I never wanted to leave.

CHADD

"Chadd!" Kayla called out for me over my office intercom.

"Yeah?"

"Don't forget you have that meeting with John in ten minutes," she reminded me.

There I was still working like a regular person, as if my wife wasn't still in the hands of one of the most dangerous men known to mankind.

"Okay, thanks," I told her and clicked off the phone.

It had been about two months since I gave him the large payment; all I owed him was one million. On several occasions, I'd tried to reach him, so I could give him the rest of the money, but he'd been dodging my calls and it wasn't like I knew where the man lived or worked.

As days went by, I became more and more stressed, worried, and afraid. It just didn't make sense for a man that wanted all his money and was able to get it to just go ghost. It had me thinking all sorts of shit like something happened to Lyric, which I prayed every day she was safe and unharmed. With no answer from him or no pop-up visits from his son, it was just a waiting game on my end, one I hoped ended as soon as possible.

My phone chimed, pulling me from my thoughts of Lyric and the situation. When I looked, it was John.

John: You ready? Let's go kill this proposal and get this client!

Me: Always ready, let's do it!

I gathered my stuff for the meeting and left my office. On my way out, I rested some things on Kayla's desk for her to handle for me.

Kayla was starting to show a little bump due to her small size, but she kept wearing loose-fitting clothes, so no one jumped in her face to be nosy. As far as everyone at the firm knew, Kayla was a single hard-working woman, so her popping up pregnant would prompt everyone to start asking questions, some in good faith while others just liked to pry.

On my way to the conference room, I saw Kayla speaking to another co-worker. When she saw me, she pulled her cardigan closed and continued her conversation. I went about my business as usual, trying not to make things obvious between the two of us.

"Heyyy, there he is!" John yelled when I walked into the room.

The two potential clients were already there and seated.

"Good afternoon, everyone," I greeted with a smile. I went over to shake both the man and woman, who were husband and wife, hands.

"I'm Chadd Larson, pleasure to meet you," I said as I took the husband's hand into mine.

"I'm Chris Levi, and this is my wife, Nicole Levi," he spoke back. "So, you're the big shot guy around here I've been hearing about, huh?" he stated.

"Who, me?" I rested my hand on my chest, pretending to be in fake disbelief.

Everyone started to laugh, making the mood in the room light and easy to work in.

"I'm just some guy who's good with numbers, that's all." I smiled and winked.

"Well, guy that's good with numbers, please show us what you can do," Mrs. Levi spoke up and stated.

Not wasting any time, both John and I jumped into our presentation we worked on specifically for the Levi's. While we took turns speaking and explaining things, the couple nodded and seemed to be impressed, something I expected of course.

There was no denying my ability to make people more money. I had a gift for numbers, I knew it since I was a kid. Proving it to clients was the hard part. Some people would take word of mouth and sign on with me, while others wanted to see the number, stats, and my success track record.

"So, that is our presentation designed just for you," John concluded.

The Levi's clapped and smiled.

"Nice work, guys," Mr. Levi exclaimed.

"Thank you, Sir," John and I said in a unison.

"But, there's one thing before we feel a hundred percent comfortable placing our money in your hands," Mrs. Levi stated.

"And what's that?" John questioned.

"You two married, correct?" she asked.

We both answered yes.

"Well, I would love for us all to have dinner together, your wives included."

When those words left her mouth, my heart dropped to the pit of my stomach. "Why, may I ask?" I wondered.

"While this is business for you, it's personal for us. I want to make sure we're making the right decision when picking you to handle our accounts. You can tell a lot about a man by the way they treat their significant other and act around them," she explained.

Well, you'll be able to tell I'm a fraud of a husband, I thought to myself.

"That's no problem at all, Mrs. Levi. We'd love to join you guys for dinner," John offered our acceptance of their invitation.

"Great, we'll sort out the details later," Mr. Levi said as he stood to his feet.

The couple shook our hands and left the conference room, along with John, leaving me to wonder how the hell I was going to pull things off.

THE REST OF THE WORK DAY WAS A BLUR. JUST WHEN I thought I had things under control, reality smacked me in the face, showing me that wasn't the case. When I was on my way out the office, Kayla stopped me.

"I need money to go shopping for clothes. I keep wearing the same shit over and over again, and most of my things are starting not to fit," she complained.

Without saying a word, I turned around and went right back into my office with her following me close behind. I went into my wallet and saw I only had a few hundred on me.

"Here, take this for now. I'll go to the ATM and drop off some more money to you," I told her as I handed over the money.

"Thank you," she said in a childlike tone.

"Mmmhmmm."

Things between Kayla and I became rough over the past two months. She started being extra clingy, bossy, and always emotional. I knew it was the hormones, but I felt she was using that as an excuse and to her advantage.

Out of everyone, she was the only person who really knew

what was going on. She knew firsthand that my mental wasn't right and that I was uneasy with Lyric being gone. I didn't know why I thought she'd have any kind of sense and compassion. At the end of the day, she probably would've loved to see Lyric out the picture completely.

After I gave her the money, I left the office and made my way home. I started back staying at the house since it would've definitely looked unusual if I hadn't. It was already bad enough Lyric wasn't around and I knew people were speculating things.

Once I was close to the house, I stopped at the bank and pulled some money from the ATM. I had planned on going home, shower, get something to eat, and then drop off the remaining money I had to give Kayla.

As I reached home and got out the car, I waved at Mrs. Lawrence from across the street and headed inside. Walking through the house, I cringed at the untidiness of the place but, for some reason, I just couldn't pull myself out of the funk to clean it up. Lyric used to have the house clean, looking and smelling good. I wouldn't say I was a messy or nasty person, I just wasn't in the right state of mind to do anything that I felt wasn't a necessity at the time.

I quickly went in the shower, washed my skin, rinsed, and got out. I threw on a sweatsuit and made my way downstairs to the kitchen. When I opened the fridge door, I was staring at an empty refrigerator. I opened the freezer and saw it had two frozen meals inside. That's when I decided I was going to grab something to eat while I was outside.

I turned, left out the kitchen and headed for the front door. The moment I opened it, I was hit with a surprise.

"Hello, Chadd," Lori-Ann said with an evil grin on her face. She was accompanied by Nick, of course.

"Hi, Lori-Ann," I greeted her. "Nick." I nodded in his direction.

"Mmmhmmm," Nick hummed with an irritated expression on his face.

"Listen, where's my sister? We haven't heard from her for months and that ain't like her," Lori-Ann pushed.

"I told you, she took some time for herself. I assure you she's fine," I lied.

"Bullshit, Chadd!" Nick raised his voice.

"Have you called her phone?" I asked them.

"Yes, and now it just goes to voicemail like it's off or something," Lori-Ann stated.

"I spoke with her last week. When I speak to her again, I'll tell her to contact you guys. I've told her this before though."

"He's fuckin' lying Lori," Nick snapped.

"Calm down, Nick. If he is, the truth will come to the light, best believe that," she said, staring straight into my eyes.

Trying my best to keep my poker face and not give away anything, I stared right back into her eyes. "I was heading out so, if you two don't mind, excuse me." I stepped out the house, closed the front door, and locked it.

As I was walking to my car, they started to go towards theirs, which was blocking me in.

"Since you won't give us proper answers, we'll get them ourselves," Lori-Ann exclaimed.

I wasn't sure what she meant by that, but I sure wasn't in the mood to ask and keep the conversation going. Nodding my head, I saluted them and got in my car.

Without having to ask or even beep a horn, they drove off, so I was able to back out the driveway and go about my way. As I was driving, I couldn't stop replaying the scene that just occurred. I knew they could've brought potential trouble to my doorstep, so I had to take actions. I searched for Mr. Luchiano's number in my phone and hit the call button next to it.

As expected, it rang out and went to voicemail. I tried back two more times and got the same results but, the last time, I decided to leave a voicemail.

"Hello, Mr. Luchiano, it's Chadd. I've been trying to reach you countless times. I'm not sure what the holdup is, but I'd like to get back what is rightfully mine. I have the rest of the stuff for you and been trying to get it to you. Please, many questions are being asked and we don't need anyone snooping. Contact me back at you earliest convenience. Thank you."

I hung up and took a deep breath, letting it out slowly.

Please lord, let this man call me back soon, I prayed.

CHAPTER 4

LORENZO "DON LUCHI" LUCHIANO

Knock! Knock!

"Mmm," the nice young lady moaned while she slurped my dick.

Knock! Knock!

There someone was again at my office door, once again. "Who is it?" I yelled out.

"It's Phil, Boss," he answered.

"You want me to stop, daddy?" my treat asked.

"No, continue sugar." I guided her head back down my manhood. "Come in, Phil," I instructed him."

When he walked in, he obviously knew what I had going on, so he stayed near the door.

"What's so damn urgent you couldn't wait until I was done?" I questioned him.

"The Larson kid keeps calling but, this time, he left a voice-mail, one that should concern us," he informed me.

"Sweetheart." I looked down at the girl.

"Huh?" she asked with lustful eyes.

"Close your mouth and get out until I'm ready for you again."

With the quickness, she jumped to her feet and sped out the office pass Phil. Not having to tell him anything, he closed the door behind her and waited a second for me to cover myself.

"Now, what's the problem?" I queried.

"Listen to this." He clicked the voicemail on one of my business phones he handled.

What I heard sounded like a poor kid just begging for his wife back. But, then again, I knew it had to be some truth to what he was saying. Lyric had been taken from him for months and, when he thought she was about to be returned to him, it didn't happened.

After all the time that had passed, I wasn't surprised people started looking for her. She wasn't a low-key kind of person. Being an author meant she had to be in the spotlight and active, which she wasn't.

"So, what we going to do?" Phil pressed.

"We need to get her back and to him. I'm not sure how much longer that kid can keep his mouth shut. If everything comes crashing down on him, he'll start to sing like a bird and I'll really have to kill him."

"Understood."

"Find Logan's location, by any means necessary," I ordered.

Phil turned on his heels and started to leave out the door until I stopped him. "Send my treat back in here, please and thank you," I told him.

As he left out, the young lady strutted her way back in and came right back between my legs to finish what she was doing. Sliding down my slacks, she pulled my dick out my boxer briefs and swallowed it whole. I leaned my head back and enjoyed the pleasure she was giving me; it had been a while since I felt that way.

After the whole shit went down the night Cat and my secret got out, I'd been to myself trying to strategize what to do next. My relationship with my son was broken, Cat and I were on the outs, which she wanted, and her father and I weren't on good terms, which started messing with money.

Catteleya's father, Raphael De León, and I had a good business relationship going. My product and weapons passed through his territory in Mexico and, in exchange, he got paid and also got a good deal off the product for himself.

Once he learned of his daughter's scandalous ways and who she'd been having them with, he couldn't bear to look at her. Immediately, he cut her off and me as well, but I had high hopes we could rekindle our business and continue to make money together.

When it came to my son, Logan, that was a different story. I loved him with everything in me, but he did the unthinkable and fucked with my business. I was always a man of my word so if I told someone I was going to do something, it happened, no questions asked.

Since Logan decided he wanted to run off with the next man's wife, I was placed in a sticky situation that not only made me look like I couldn't be trusted, but may cause attention to shift my way. I'd always moved quietly with little to no one knowing what I did, where I was, or who even knew me. Staying low was how I survived for years as the head of a mob. If it was one thing my father taught me, he made sure I knew how to move properly.

Logan was putting everything at risk and, for that, I couldn't let it slide. Son or not, he went against my orders, and I couldn't tolerate that. There was going to be consequences one way or another.

I thought I wanted the sweet thing to come and finish but, after hearing the voicemail and noticing the importance of the issue at hand, I couldn't even concentrate on releasing myself.

"It's okay, love. Leave me alone, I'll call you later, maybe," I told her.

Knowing better, she got up like last time and didn't utter a word. She just fixed her clothes and left my office. I didn't even know her name; she was just someone I met at a bar a week before. I'd been paying her some money to keep me happy sexually, no strings attached.

Getting up from my chair behind my desk, I went into the bathroom that was adjacent to the office and cleaned myself off. When I walked back to my desk, I looked at the clock on my wall and saw it was just about time for dinner. I wrapped up what I was doing before I had her come in and headed out the office and into the dining area.

While I was sitting at the table alone, my thoughts started to drown me once again. Life was moving so smoothly and, within a snap of a second, it changed. I had to do damage control and fast before things got worst. I couldn't afford to look weak, not with so many people following my lead and especially not with outsiders, Catteleya's father, to be exact.

"Boss." Phil walked into the dining room.

"Yes." I looked at him in annoyance but was also grateful he snapped me out of it.

"I had the kid in IT hack into the neighbor's camera and look." He placed the phone on the table in front of me.

There were two people, a man and a woman, at the front door of Chadd's. They had seemed to be in a heated debate and that was what probably caused him to call me with so much urgency in his voice. My guess was it was Lyric's friends or family.

"So, he really is panicking for some reason," I concluded as I sat back in my seat.

"Yeah, whoever they are must be asking questions. And you know it's not long until they get the police involved. It's no telling what Chadd will say or do." Phil made a point.

I nodded in agreement because everything he stated was true. "We have to find them," I said above a whisper and to no one in particular.

I WAS OUTSIDE BY THE POOLSIDE ENJOYING MY afternoon lunch and the fresh air when I was rudely interrupted.

"Sir, you have a visitor, and she said she isn't leaving until she sees you," one of my men informed me.

Popping a grape in my mouth and then a sip of my mimosa, I took a deep breath because I had an idea who it was. "Who is it?" I asked, just to confirm.

"Catteleya, Sir," he answered.

Just as I predicted, it was her indeed. She'd been coming by the house time and time again, trying to see me. I just felt it was no need to deal with her, or at least at that moment. Too much had transpired and I didn't need additional damage being done, something I should've thought of earlier.

Maybe I should've just let her go when she asked, I thought.

"Let her in." I waved him off.

I tried to eat as much of my food that I was able to before she reached me. Who knew what kind of mood I was going to be put in with her energy; I wasn't sure what she needed to see me about.

Not long after the guard left, he returned with her trailing behind him. I couldn't lie, she looked beautiful and had no stress in sight, even though I knew she was going through a lot.

"Here she is, Sir," he announced and stepped aside for her to walk up to me.

I motioned for her to take a seat while I finished up my meal.

"Hi, Lorenzo," she finally spoke up.

"What do you want, Cat?" I asked her straight up.

"I need you to make things right with my father. If he gets back on the right track with you, it will be room for forgiveness for me. You get what I mean?" she pleaded.

I took a minute to process what she was asking. While I already had plans on trying to fix things with her father, I didn't think I'd be meddling in father-daughter affairs.

"I'll speak to your father, or at least try to. I can't promise anything. I don't know how I'd act myself if my daughter was fooling around with my business partner who is also my son-in-law's father."

"Yeah, just rub it in," she spat and rolled her eyes.

"You done here?" I looked at her closely.

"As a matter of fact, I am. Fuck you, Renzo." She got up and stormed away from the pool side.

I debated on if I should've gave things more time before calling De León or just try my luck. After some thought, I decided to just pick up my phone and call the man. It was time we had that conversation that had been brewing.

Finally locating his number in my phone, I pressed call and let it ring. It rang a good number of times to where I thought he wasn't going to answer. When I was just about to hang up, he answered.

"What do I owe this pleasure?" he asked in his thick Spanish accent.

"De León, we need to talk," I exclaimed.

The phone went silent for a few seconds.

"Well, talk."

Being the boss I was, it took all of me not to say something rude back. I had to remember the reason I was calling and figured I needed to be the bigger person.

"We need to sort things out. All the personal is bad for business, clearly," I exclaimed.

Instead of responding or even giving a grunt, he stayed silent, so I continued to speak, hoping to make him answer or at least say a word.

"I know my side of the business isn't the only one getting hit, yours has to be as well. So, what will it take for us to try to get things back rolling?" I just came out and asked.

He coughed and cleared his throat. "You've disgraced my family, amigo. And yet you come to me about business before even apologizing? No," he stated and hung up the phone.

I felt myself getting angry and ready to kill anything in sight. My nose flared up as my body started to become hot. I stood to my feet and threw my phone into the pool with so much force; I was sure it broke before even hitting the water. One thing I didn't take well was disrespect and rejection, it never ended well, especially for the other party involved.

"Boss!" I heard Phil yell from a distance.

What the fuck now? I thought to myself. If it was not one thing, it was the next.

I didn't even answer him since I was still upset about how the phone call went with De León. When he finally reached and stood right in front of me, I noticed he was wearing a menacing grin on his face.

"We found them," he announced.

CHAPTER 5

LOGAN

S ome time had passed, and things were going great with Lyric and me. Shorty was a whole vibe, a vibe I didn't know I needed. Being around her was so comforting, physically and emotionally. Chadd definitely fumbled a good one, but I was glad he did or else I wouldn't have been able to show her what a real nigga looked like.

As for everything else, it had been quiet. Our location had been secured without any problems, and my guys were on high alert around the clock. Although I hadn't heard anything from my father or even Cat's father, I knew something was brewing and it was only a matter of time until shit would hit the fan. But, until then, I was enjoying my peace of mind and quality time with Lyric.

Lyric had been working hard when it came to therapy to strengthen her hand. One main reason besides wanting to be able to use her hand like she normally did was that it was her writing hand that was broken. Day in and day out, she would constantly remind me that she needed to be able to write; it was the one thing that kept her sane, especially being couped up in the house every day. The furthest she went was to the beach, and I was either with her or a guard or two.

"Ahhh shit!" I heard Lyric yell out loud from downstairs after the sound of a broken glass hit the floor.

I was in the bed just relaxing when she said she was thirsty. Just when I was about to climb out of bed, she stopped me and told me she'd do it, that she wasn't handicap, so I let her.

Running downstairs, of course, before I got to her, one of the guys did. Once he saw it wasn't anything serious and I waved him off, he went back to his post.

"You aight, baby?" I asked her.

Lyric was hold her hands to her face, looking stressed. "I'm fine, I'm fine," she sighed out loud.

"What happened?"

"I-I- um- just had a flashback. I'm okay," she tried to water down the situation.

She had been getting nightmares and flashbacks since she woke up out the coma. The events that haunted her was from initially being taken and the accident.

"You sure?" I walked up and pulled her in close to me.

She nodded her head against my chest and wrapped her

arms around me tightly. I kissed her on the forehead and cupped her head close to me.

"Go upstairs. let me clean this up real quick and I'll bring you something to drink," I told her.

"Okay," she spoke softly.

When she walked away, I went ahead and started cleaning up the mess, taking my time so I wouldn't get cut.

It was still early on in the day and still had much more time before the night came around. Knowing all that she was going through, I bussed my brain to see what I could've done to make her smile and feel special. I wanted to take her mind off things, even if it was temporary.

By the time I was finished cleaning up, it came to me. I grabbed my phone out the pocket of my basketball shorts and called the private chef I had on payroll since we been at the beach house. I told him I needed a special meal for the night and I'd like his event planning service he offered. That night, I wanted to do something a little different.

After I put things in place and told Joe all about it, I went back upstairs with the cup in hand, filled with juice for Lyric. She was in the bed, cuddled up under the sheets watching one of her ratchet TV shows she had been forcing me to watch with her.

Just to keep her out the way and distracted, I hopped in bed with her and watched whatever it was she wanted to watch. Anytime she wanted something, I jumped up before she could and got it for her. All while keeping her busy, I was texting back and forth with Joe, the chef, and his event planner he was partnered with.

I had the planner go and grab Lyric a pretty dress to wear for the occasion that night. Joe was making sure things were calm around the house as usual, as well as keeping track of the planner while she decorated and all that good shit.

Before I knew it, I received a text saying to start getting her ready. I slipped out the room and went and got the dress, amongst other things she got for her, and returned to the room.

"What's that?" Lyric asked as soon as I walked back through the door.

Damn, women could be hella nosy sometimes, I thought to myself.

"Something for you." I smiled, walking up to her.

She beamed and hadn't even seen the contents inside the bag yet. Once I handed it over to her, she didn't waste a second before taking the things out. One by one, as she took each item out, her eyes grew wide with excitement.

"Baby, this is so beautiful," she squealed, looking at the stuff. "But, why?" She looked at me with a confused face.

"Go get showered up and get ready, don't ask me nothing else," I instructed.

Lyric jumped off the bed like a big kid and ran to me. "Thank you." She kissed my lips.

"Don't thank me just yet," I smirked.

While she hopped in the shower, I ran downstairs to see how everything was coming along. Satisfied with what I saw, I went ahead and handled my own hygiene and got ready.

About an hour later, Lyric was finally ready. The moment I laid eyes on her, a nigga got weak. She was gorgeous from head to toe, and I knew she was feeling herself because she couldn't stop smiling.

The floral pattern dress fitted her perfectly. It was a sundress that flowed, giving her room to move around comfortably but still feel like the queen she was. She applied makeup to her face and combed her hair into a neat bun on top her head. To finish her look, she wore the jewelry that was bought for her and a cute pair of sandals that matched her dress.

"You look the fuck good," I blurted out.

"Really? Bae?" she rolled her eyes.

"My fault but damn." I walked towards her. "You look beautiful, baby," I corrected myself as I wrapped my arms around all that voluptuous curves she had.

"Thank you," she cooed with a bright smile.

I took her hand, led her out the room and down the stairs.

"Where are we going? What's going on Logan?" she kept rattling off question after question.

"Chill, man. Relax yourself," I told her.

She huffed out loud and decided to stay quiet.

Walking through the house, we bypassed everything and made our way to the sliding glass door that led to the beach. When we stepped outside and started walking towards the water, I felt her hands tighten the grip on mine.

"No," she whispered in disbelief.

I looked down at her, and she had her free hand covering her mouth. That's when the cat was out the bag.

The whole romantic set-up was a straight vibe. They made us a pillow-themed dinner set up with a table for the food of course. There were rose petals and candles leading up to the area and a band playing soft jazz music. The sun was setting, making the moment and scene even more beautiful.

Lyric let go of my hand and now had both of her hands covering her mouth. I saw her eyes becoming watery with every step she took and got closer.

"Logan," she whined.

"You like?" I asked in a humor-like tone.

"What?" she raised her voice. "What kind of question is that? I love it." She turned to me and hugged me tight as ever. Reaching up on her tippy toes, she puckered her lips for a kiss, but I didn't meet her halfway.

"A nigga gon' need more than a kiss. After all this, you better bounce that ass all over my dick tonight," I joked.

"And that I will," she assured me and smiled.

I reached down and finally gave her the kiss she was looking for. We stepped around the pillows, sat down, and got comfortable. The chef came and uncovered our plates, exposing a delicious smelling and looking meal. If you'd ask me what it was, I would've told you a lie because it was some fantasy shit.

The night went as planned; Lyric couldn't keep the smile off her face, and I wouldn't have had it any other way. My queen was happy and, even if it was for the moment, I took it all in and enjoyed it. I prayed we got out of the situation we were in and continued to have more memorable times.

AFTER OUR ROMANTIC DINNER ON THE BEACH, OF course, we took things back to the room and enjoyed each other for desserts. Round after round left both of us exhausted and knocked out.

In the middle of the night, I woke up feeling parched. I gently slid out of bed, making sure not to wake Lyric, and went downstairs to the kitchen. While on my way down the stairs, I heard someone whispering as if they were having a conversation, so I continued to walk lightly.

"I'm ready when you are," the person said.

When I finally reached the bottom of the staircase, I quietly moved about towards the voice. Breaking the corner, I saw it was one of my guards who'd been with us for a short period of time, just hanging up the phone. While I was paranoid and on high alert with every little thing, I also didn't want to jump to conclusions about anything. The dude could've simply been having a quick conversation with his girl or something. I wasn't fancy with the whole phone thing but, I knew at the end of the day, these guys were a part of a family. I just trusted that they used their devices appropriately and didn't betray my trust in any sort of way.

"Oh, Boss, sorry, I was just—"

I lifted my hand up to silence him. "It's cool, just make sure the same way you paying attention to that phone, you paying attention to this house and everything that moves around it," I advised him.

"Yes, Sir." He nodded.

"Good."

I walked off and left him standing in the same spot as I continued into the kitchen. Grabbing the bottle of apple juice and a glass, I poured a good bit and gulped it down.

Since my thirst was quenched, I made my way back upstairs and into bed. After what felt like only a few minutes, Lyric rolled over and slightly woke up. Apparently, I wasn't the only one thirsty that night.

"I'm going to get something to drink," she told me as she got out the bed.

"You sure you don't want me go and get it?" I sat up.

"I'm fine, bae. Let me stretch these legs of mine." She waved me off like an old woman would.

"I think I'm finna get a damn mini fridge in here," I joked, as she walked out the room laughing.

She was laughing, but I was dead ass serious. The way we always wanted something to drink was ridiculous. I laid back in the bed and got comfortable. As I was closing my eyes for a split second, I felt the tip of a silencer in the back of my head.

"Your father sends his regards," the familiar voice said.

At that moment, I knew my life was over, so there was no point in fighting. He caught me with my dick in my hand, lacking.

The sound of a silencer went off, but I wasn't hit and still alive. A body dropped to the ground, making a loud thud. I slowly turned around to see Joe standing there pointing his gun at a dead nigga on the floor.

As I was swinging my legs around to plant my feet on the floor, I looked closer and saw it was the same guy I caught on the phone earlier. "Where's Lyric?" I asked in a panic.

I grabbed my gun and silencer from the nightstand drawer and mounted them together, as Joe and I slowly walked out the room. Moving quickly but quietly, we tip-toed down the stairs and into the living room, then the kitchen. Lyric was nowhere in sight, and I started to feel uneasy.

When I turned around in the direction of the beach, I saw Lyric being dragged away by someone. "Joe!" I yelled.

He ran into the kitchen, ready to shoot something.

"They got her." I rushed to the sliding door and out into the cool spring air.

With all my might, I picked my feet up as fast as I could to get to Lyric. The sand alone slowed us down a bit, but we didn't allow it to hold us back too much.

Looking far into the distance, it was only one person with Lyric. She tried her all to fight him off, but he used his gun to his advantage and kept it trained on her.

Catching up to the two of them, I said a silent prayer that he didn't shoot her; I would've rather it be me to take a bullet if any one of us had to.

"Let her go, man!" I yelled, as we reached them.

I realized it was one of my guys again, which was when everything made sense to me. My father somehow got to my men and had them turn on me. If he came in blazing, he knew it wouldn't been an all-out bloodbath with a potential of killing Lyric, and that couldn't happen.

She was the prize in it all; he wanted her returned to her dickhead of a husband. My father had a bad problem when it came to not having his way. If he gave a word on something, in his eyes, it must happen one way or another.

"I have to get her back to Don Luchi or else he'll kill my family," he pleaded.

"Nigga, what the fuck you think I'll do to you?" I spat. The way he had his gun pointed at her head made me foam at the mouth. I was ready to pounce on his bitch ass with my bare hands.

"I'm taking the shot when it's clear," Joe whispered loud enough for me to hear.

I nodded my head, giving him the green light. Joe had precise aim and was a beast when it came to putting down muthafuckers, so I trusted that he'd take him out and leave Lyric unharmed.

"You got five seconds to drop your gun and let her go," I told him. He continued to backpedal with Lyric in his arms and gun pointed at her head. "Five, four, three, two—"

Pew! Pew!

His body dropped dead to the sand on the spot. Lyric ran into my arms, as Joe went and checked his pulse.

"He's out," he confirmed.

"You good, ma?" I asked her as I held her face in my hands.

"I thought I was dead," she cried.

"Me too," I whispered as I pulled her in close.

"We have to move and now. Who knows how many of them

are sitting around the perimeter or who else he got to?" Joe exclaimed.

He had a point. While I'd love to have an army around me in that moment, it wasn't smart because we weren't sure who was loyal. The only people I trusted were Joe and Lyric, so those were the two who I had to figure shit out with.

We quickly made our way back into the house and tried our best to stay quiet. The other men were still walking around the house and one was positioned upstairs in the attic.

"Do you need anything from the room? Only if it's important, Lyric," I asked her.

"My books, they're in the drawer on the nightstand near the window."

"Take her to the SUV," I instructed Joe.

Joe and I prepared for situations like this particular one. We had the money, important documents, and other necessities already in the trunk of the truck. No one but he and I knew the things were in there, not even Lyric.

It was supposed to be a hop in the vee and dip kind of move, but I knew how much those books meant to Lyric, so I risked my life to go and get them for her.

Moving swiftly, I reached the room and went straight for the drawer. Just like she said, the books were sitting right in there. I grabbed them up but, by the time I lifted my head up, I caught a bullet in my arm, making me drop to the floor immediately.

"Shiiittt," I hissed. "I'ma kill you, muthafucker."

"I'd like to see you try, but I will make sure and get the job done for your daddy," the person taunted.

Holding my wounded arm, I felt a stinging pain that made it hard for me to move my arm. I tucked Lyric's books in between my bad arm and side, making sure to press down on them so they wouldn't fall.

Looking from under the bed, I saw he was still right outside the door. Every other second, he would look inside and, every time he did, his right foot would point inside the room.

With a couple of deep breaths, I kissed my Glock and, with all the strength I had, I rose up and waited for him to poke his head in the door. The moment he did, I sent one single bullet in the center of his forehead.

Not trying to waste another second for another person to come after me, or even Joe and Lyric, I dashed out the room and down the stairs. I ran fast as I could to the door that led to the garage where the truck was parked. Once I opened it, I quickly made my way to the front to make sure they were good and it wasn't another set-up.

Both Joe and Lyric were alive and safe, so I hopped in the backseat, and Joe opened the garage door to get us out of there.

"Baby, you're shot!" Lyric yelled.

"Is it bad?" Joe asked.

"I'm good, man, just drive," I growled.

"Where are we even going?" Lyric questioned with much concern in her voice.

"To a place I shouldn't have probably never left."

"Stop right here," I told Joe, as he pulled over near a corner.

We had just arrived to my old neighborhood, Queensbridge, the very place I was born and raised with my mother, until she was taken away from me. The place was still with barely any movements. It was about four in the morning, so the only people who were awake were the either the hustlers, fiends, or regular individuals who worked the graveyard shift.

"You see that corner store right there?" I pointed in the direction of what I was speaking about.

"Yeah," he answered.

"Go to the window, tell the person to call Tione and tell him 4123-05," I instructed.

Without asking any questions, Joe hopped out the truck and went to the store. Lyric was wide awake and applying pressure to my gun wound, which had my arm numb at that point. I knew I'd survive it, so it was nothing to trip about but, leave it to Lyric, she was acting like I was seconds away from checking.

Moments later, Joe returned to the truck and sat back behind the wheel.

"What's good?" I asked.

"He said to go to the building, whatever that means." He shrugged.

I knew exactly what that meant. "Make this left," I told him.

He place the vee in drive and bussed the left. I directed him on where to go and, when we reached it, he found a perfect parking spot right near the building entrance.

Just when we parked up, two guys came walking out the building and towards the truck.

"You know them?" Joe asked, staring at the men closely.

"No, but they're friendly," I assured him.

"Better be." I saw him touch his waist to feel his gun.

When they reached the vehicle, Joe lowered the window for me.

"Lo?" one stepped up and asked.

"Yeah," I answered.

"Come on," he simply said.

Joe put the window back up, and we all climbed out the truck. I told him to grab the bags and what he needed extra hands for, the guys helped out with.

We followed them into the building and then into the small elevator. When we reached the fourth floor, everyone got off and damn near at the same time let out a deep breath. One thing that hadn't changed from back in the days were the pissy ass halls and elevators. I believe even if NYCHA tried to clean the place, it just wouldn't have taken away the stench; it was deeply rooted.

Stopping in front an apartment, one of the guys opened the door, allowing us entry and followed us inside.

"Make yourself comfortable. I'll get the doctor over here for you," the same one who spoke up first stated. "Tione will be here in a few hours; he told me to relay the message."

I nodded and grabbed ahold of Lyric's hand, as we went and sat on the couch. The place was nicely furnished and well kept. I wouldn't lie and say I knew it would've been like that, I didn't.

Tione was a street kingpin, so I automatically thought we were about to be held up in one of his trap houses in the buildings, but I assumed wrong.

Joe didn't take a seat; instead, he made his rounds around the apartment as soon as they guys stepped out. Lyric was still attached to my arm like it was going to fall off if she didn't hold onto it. And I was just tired and in need of rest, but I knew sleep was nowhere in the near future for me.

About an hour went by, and the doctor finally arrived. He was an older black gentleman. Before he even asked me what happened and how it happened, he gave me painkillers to take. At that time, my arm went from numb to having its own heartbeat, so I was grateful for the relief method.

Once I told him what went down, of course not detailed but where and how I was hit, he knew how to proceed. Within an hour, I was patched and cleaned up. The bullet was out, and the wound was in good shape.

"Make sure you take these antibiotics until it's finished," he instructed as he handed me a bottle of meds. "And do me a favor and keep his wound clean. Change his dressing once you see even a peck of bleed," he turned to Lyric and told her.

"Yes, Sir. Thank you so much," she thanked him.

"Yeah, doc, I appreciate this."

"Just doing my job. I'm glad you're okay son." He smiled and grabbed up his things to leave.

I wasn't sure what time Tione had planned on coming, but I decided to go and take a little snooze until he did. Joe was wide awake, so I took advantage of that and got some shut eye for a few, so did Lyric.

~

KNOCK! KNOCK!

"Logan, your people's here to see you." Joe poked his head in the room.

I jumped up and saw Lyric was knocked out, but what I couldn't wrap my head around was how the hell did I end up in the room when I fell asleep on the couch?

Shaking off my thoughts, I saw the duffle bag in the corner; I went and grabbed a black Polo t-shirt out of it and took my time putting it on. When I walked outside the door and into the living room, there was a dripped-out Tione.

"This tall muthafucker, man. I swear yo ass should've been in the NBA all now," Tione cracked.

"Antione muthafucking James," I exclaimed as I clapped my hands. We met halfway and had a warm brotherly embrace.

Antione, known as Tione or Touchi, was the man around the way. He ran everything from the gangs, drugs, and scams throughout Queens and other parts of New York. We were boys from birth basically. Grew up running around the projects together, went to school and all with each other at a point too. Our mothers were close, so it was only right we were.

"Damn, I missed you, my boy," he confessed when we broke our embrace.

"I missed you as well, nigga."

We hadn't seen or spoken to each other in years, ever since I went to live with my father full-time as a matter of fact. I had to leave my old life behind, orders from my father, which in some way I felt was the best decision.

The way the mob was set up, it was best to keep your circle small, that way no one would've been able to use anyone against you. I didn't want to put Tione or anyone else I used to run the streets with in harm's way, so I did what my ops said.

"Doc got you straight I see." He pointed at my arm.

"Facts, he did his thing, appreciate that."

"No doubt. When you left and I told you no matter what, home is home and I will always have your back, didn't I?" he reminded me.

"You sure did, nigga. That's exactly why I felt comfortable enough to come here," I voiced.

"I know it got to be some shit going on for you to be here," he pried.

"Yeah, it's some shit alright." I finally plopped down on the coach.

"Well, whatever it is, I'm riding and ain't shit changing that," he reassured.

Tione was as loyal as they came; he'd always been that way since a kid. He was the type of nigga I could've put my head on a block and get it chopped off for him, that's how well I knew him.

I started to think I should have never left him behind. I made a mental note, when and if I got out of the situation alive, I wasn't ever disconnecting with my brother again.

CHAPTER 6

LYRIC

My life flashed before me once again, something that had been happening more often than it ever should. I didn't know what I did in the past to be having this much backlash, I knew it couldn't have been my karma. Not to say I was perfect, but I always did right by people for the most part; I was always the one getting fucked over.

I had a gun pointed at me one too many times and it was sad to say; after the last time, I was numb to it. The shit didn't faze me. Going to church every Sunday was something I did when I was younger. When I grew up, it slowed down but my beliefs never left me. I was a strong believer in when it was my time to go and God called my number, then that's what it was; you couldn't fight fate.

Although we were on the run, the beach house was a nice set up Logan had for us. I couldn't go anywhere, but at least I still had the beautiful view of the waves crashing against the shore and I was able to take walks out onto the sand. Now, I was staring outside an apartment window located in a projects.

There was no waves, no fresh breeze, seagulls flying around; all I saw was concrete floors, benches, and trash all over the ground, and I heard loud chatter from people, car horns and engines.

"Baby," Lo came into the room and startled me.

"Shit, Lo." I held my chest.

"My fault. I ain't even know you were up, that's why I came in quiet."

"It's cool. Wassup? Everything alright?" I searched his face for any concern.

"Nah, everything good. I was just chopping it up with my mans, catching up and shit."

"Who is this person exactly?" I raised a brow.

He walked over to me and grabbed my hand, sitting me down on the bed next to him. "My boy name is Tione. We grew up together but, after my mom passed and my father took me full-time, I had to leave my old life here behind. I didn't want to but it was more so for his and my other friends' protection," he explained.

"Oh, I see. Well, if you're able to access him like you did early this morning, he's someone you need not to leave behind anymore," I voiced.

He nodded his head and seemed to quickly sink into a deep thought, then snapped out of it.

"It's a bacon, egg, and cheese on a bagel for you; you want it?" he asked with a smirk.

"Hell yeah, bring that joint," I beamed.

Not only was I hungry, but I missed the good ol' fashion corner store bacon, egg, and cheese. Staten Island didn't have nothing on stores like in Brooklyn, Queens, or even the Bronx; the taste was just different.

Lo left out the room and returned within seconds holding the sandwich and a strawberry Arizona in his hand.

My kind of guy, I thought.

Unwrapping the fine art of a meal, I hurriedly took a bite as if it would disappear any minute. "Mmmm, this is so good," I cheesed.

"I already know, I fucked mine up."

We both laughed.

"Bae, where's Joe?" I wondered.

"He's resting, finally. I had to damn near beg the nigga to close his eyes." He shook his head.

I didn't blame Joe for how he felt and how he moved. Knowing he had been working with Lo's family for some time, I knew he'd seen some crazy shit. He was the type of person you would have to get God to come down for him to let his guard down all the way. He probably was in the room sleep with his gun off safety and his finger on the trigger.

"Good, because he needs it. He does so much for you," I pointed out.

"Yeah, that's my dude for life."

I continued to demolish my food as I was on cloud nine. Lo sat by the window and just stared outside as if he was waiting to see someone pass by. Since it was his old neighborhood, I knew it had to be triggering and a lot of memories flooded his mind, so I gave him his space.

Once I was finished eating, I changed his dressing and bandage, made sure he took his meds, and went to handle my hygiene. By the time I came out, Joe was up and about doing the same thing Lo was doing, staring out the window but in the living room.

While I felt safe with the two men, I just wished they'd relax for at least a second, but I knew good and well it wasn't going to happen until the dust cleared.

"You good, Joe?" I asked before making my way back into the bedroom.

He nodded. "You okay?" he asked.

I nodded and smiled.

Returning back in the room, Logan didn't move from his spot at the window.

"Looking for someone?" I joked.

He turned and snapped out of his daze when he heard me and started chuckling. "Nah, not at all. It's just a lot of memories coming back to me being here, you know?" he confessed.

"Yeah, I get it." I just sat near him in silence and allowed him to reminisce peacefully. Eventually, I ended up falling asleep once again; I was exhausted, and it showed.

When I woke up from my slumber, Logan was gone and the light outside turned dark. The only thing I saw through the window from the bed was a street light, so I knew night time had crept up on me.

I woke up to a cramping hand, not noticing I slept on my bad hand. It had been a whole day I hadn't done any exercises with my hands, so I knew that was another reason for the feeling.

Rolling out the bed, I left the room and went to go look for Logan but, when I reached the living room, I saw only Joe.

"Hey, where is he?" I asked, still trying to wake myself up fully.

"He went out with Tione," he informed me.

"Got cha." I nodded and turned back around.

I sat on the bed and started doing the exercises the doctor taught me. While moving my hand and doing reps, my mind slowly drifted into deep thought.

Did I make the right decision when I got up and left with Lo? What if I stayed and been back with Chadd and things would've been different for us? Did I act too soon? I asked myself.

So many thoughts were running through my mind, I couldn't even concentrate on one for a good second. It wasn't just about me anymore; I was carrying life inside of me, and every single decision I made would've affected them directly or indirectly.

Once the baby became the main thing that stuck with me, I

wondered how would his or her life be with Lo and I as parents. Would we still be on the run by the time they were ready to enter the world or would we be free to live as we please, not looking over our shoulders?

I think it's time I have a serious talk with Logan.

CHADD

earing the bird chirping, I rolled over and subconsciously felt for another body next to me, but it wasn't there. I honestly didn't know if I was feeling for Lyric or Kayla. I loved the both of them dearly but, of course, my love for Lyric was different. Now, things were definitely changing between Kayla and me since she was carrying my child.

I reached and grabbed my phone off the nightstand to notice it wasn't even time for me to get up yet. While I wanted to go back to sleep, I decided against it and just hopped up to get an early start on my day.

Since being back home, I hadn't slept in Lyric and my

bedroom; I'd been occupying the guest room, and it had been working out for me. Being in our room just didn't feel right, and I would always think about her.

Heading downstairs, I went into the kitchen to fix me a fresh pot of coffee before I started to get ready for work. Lyric usually would've been the one to get the coffee and even breakfast started for us two. It was like every single thing reminded me of her, and it messed with my mental in a bad way. That was the main reason why I didn't want to stay at the house in the first place, but it was in my best interest I started.

My coffee was finished, so I took a cup into my office and briefly looked at some emails that came in overnight. One in particular stood out to me, one of the owners of the firm said he had a few questions about an account, which was rare. The owners almost never reached out to employees like me. Granted, I was one of their highest paid workers, but they had other shit to worry about; that's why it was managers under them in place.

Quickly shooting him back an email of my schedule for the day, I got off the computer, finished my coffee, and went upstairs to get ready. Within the next hour, I was walking out the door and on my way to the office. Being that I woke up a good half an hour earlier than usual, I was ahead of the usual traffic flow, getting me to work in a fast manner.

When I walked into the office, I was the first one to arrive besides the overnight janitor getting ready to head out. I went into my office and used that time to get a head start on my pile of paperwork I had to get through.

After an hour of working, everyone started to make their way into the office, including Kayla.

"Good morning," she greeted as she walked into my office.

"Good morning." I never removed my eyes from my computer screen. I felt her still standing there, so I eventually looked up to see she had an annoyed expression on her face.

"What is it?" I quizzed.

"I was standing here showing you my stomach, but you didn't even have the common decency to look up and speak," she said in a hushed tone.

"Seriously?" I asked, scrunching up my face.

"Yes, seriously." She rolled her eyes and stormed out the office.

It's way too early for her shit, I thought.

Shaking off Kayla's bad energy early in the morning, I reverted my attention back to the screen and files on my desk.

As the day went on, I just stayed cooped up in my office getting things done. When it was time for lunch, I didn't even go out to eat; I ordered some UberEATS and had it delivered. That was another petty argument between Kayla and me. I wasn't sure why she felt I had to baby her when at the end of the day, she was a grown ass woman.

It was about two hours left before I could leave when the same owner, Steven, who emailed me, walked into my office.

"Hey, Chadd." He knocked on the opened door and invited himself in.

"Steven, what do I owe this pleasure?" I asked curiously.

"I just had to speak to you about something, nothing

major. Thanks for sending me your schedule for the day by the way, even though you were stuck to your seat the entire time."

"Yeah, had a lot to get done, didn't want anything to lapse and I fall behind. What's going on? Have a seat." I motioned for him to sit.

"No, that's fine; I'll be quick. So, we saw some unusual transactions with some of your accounts and it prompted an audit, so one will be done in the coming days. I just needed to alert you of it. An official letter stating such will be sent to you," he informed me.

My heart felt like it stopped beating while my breathing halted. I knew I couldn't show any kind of worry, so I kept it cool.

"Okay, that's fine."

"Great!" He clapped his hands together. "You enjoy the rest of your day." He turned quickly and left out.

The moment he was a good distance down the hall, Kayla ran her nosy tail in my office.

"An audit?" she asked with both eyebrows raised. "That ain't good, Chadd."

"No shit, Kayla," I snapped.

She closed the door and came and took a seat in front of me. "Any person who was ever audited ended up getting fired and also charged with something. Only about two people survived it. What did you do, Chadd?" she pushed.

I sat back in my chair and ran my hands down my face. The feeling of stress was taking over because while I always did right by the firm, I knew the Luchiano and the account I created for myself was what Steven was referring to.

"I liquidated some funds from an account I made and sent it to the guy for Lyric's return," I blurted out all in one quick breath.

"Fuck, Chadd. Fuck, fuck, fuck," Kayla hissed. "This can potentially affect me too."

She was right. As my assistant, she was hands on with a lot of things, so they'd turn to her and not only audit her assignments but ask her questions.

"Let's just keep it cool, we'll be good." I bit my bottom lip. Truth was, I was nervous as hell, but I couldn't have her panicking, especially with the baby.

We both sat there in silence for a while with nothing to say. All there was to do was wait until the audit was completed to know our fate.

ONCE STEVEN TOLD ME ABOUT THE AUDIT, I couldn't concentrate on any work at all. I tried and tried, but my mind just kept bouncing from getting fired and then to Lyric. I left earlier than I was scheduled to depart the office, but it was needed before I messed up an account while not thinking properly.

I dashed straight home with plans of just crawling into bed and shutting out the world for the rest of the day. While I just wanted to relax, people had other plans for me instead. There was a man and a woman in suits standing at my door. As I drove into my driveway, they turned and took a step down, that's when I saw their badges.

Fuck, what now? I sighed.

I cut my engine, grabbed my work bag and phone, then exited out my car.

"Mr. Larson?" the woman spoke up first.

"Yes? How may I help you?" I questioned.

"We have some questions about the whereabouts of your wife, Lyric Larson," the man stated.

"Uh huh, okay. Did her nosy sister and best friend send you here?"

"Ah, well, there was a missing person's report filed by her sister, Lori-Ann," the woman confirmed. "By the way, I'm Detective Wright and this is Detective Thomas." She pointed at her partner.

"Right. Well, like I told her sister, Lyric went on some book tour and then said she needed some space. We wasn't having the best marriage, I can admit. So, I just let her be; we speak like once a week and that's about it," I told them.

"How are you guys in contact exactly? What number does she call from?" Wright pressed.

"Her regular number, it's 347-909-1876," I recited her phone number.

She wrote everything I said down on her little pad.

"Did she mention when she was returning home?" Detective Thomas asked with an eyebrow raised.

"Not exactly, but she did say she'll be home soon," I lied.

"Hmmm, okay. Do you have a flyer or some sort of proof of this book tour she went on?"

"Uhhh, no. I didn't really meddle with her book business that much, another reason we were into it." I shrugged, making up things to say as I went.

"Alright, then. Here's our cards." They both handed me their contact cards. "It sounds like you know where she is, but we will still be trying to reach her and, if we can't, we'll be back with more questions for you," Detective Wright exclaimed.

"Sure thing, you both have a nice rest of your day now," I told them as I bypassed them to go into the house.

Shit! I said in my head as I rested against the front door once I slammed it closed. I dug in my pants pocket and got my phone, calling the one person who could make all of what was happening go away: Don Luchi.

CHAPTER 8

LOGAN

I wouldn't lie and say it wasn't hard being back home. Everything reminded me of my mother and how things used to be. We didn't have much, but we were happy and safe. Riding around the hood with Tione just showed me maybe I would've been alright if I stayed.

Tione was living his best life at the top, and it wasn't no doubt in my mind I would've been right beside him. Although I was making way more money than he was, my boy was still stacked and wasn't hurting for nothing. He even tried to put us up in the condo until I was ready to leave, but I felt a more comfort feeling being in the projects, it was like I was close to my moms or some shit.

"Yo, what ever happened to the joint Cat?" Tione blurted out and asked.

Before I responded, I just started laughing. Thankfully, I was in a space I could've done that.

"We ended up getting married, but the bitch a whole smut, fucking on my old man and shit," I put him on.

"What? See, didn't I tell you to leave that bitch where she was at that night?"

Tione was with me the night Cat and I met at the club. He had claimed she was eyeing him as well and he didn't like her vibe. I guess I should've listened to him back then, would've save me all the trouble that came with her.

"You sure enough did, my nigga." I shook my head.

"It's whatever, you happy with the joint you have now?"

"Most definitely," I answered right away without any hesitation.

"Then, that's all that matters. Fuck the past."

"Real shit," I agreed.

We had just pulled back up in from the building when I saw Joe, Lyric, and one of Tione's boys chilling outside on the bench. Lyric was rotating her hand and massaging it; I made a mental note to call up the doctor and have him come and check her out.

"Baby!" Lyric squealed when she saw me getting out the car.

The energy she gave was so refreshing. She could've saw me just an hour before and still acted like she went days or weeks without seeing me. She met me halfway as her hips moved side to side and her breasts bounced up and down.

"What's good baby girl, you good?" I moved a piece of hair that was in her face.

"I'm straight." She smiled, but it quickly disappeared to whatever it was she was looking at behind me.

Turning around swiftly, I laid eyes on my uncle Frank. Joe jumped up from his seat and stepped in front of us with his hand on his piece. Tione and a few of his guys stood on the sideway by the entrance, blocking him.

"I come in peace." He lifted his hands up in surrender.

I shot Tione a head nod, indicating it was cool. His boys patted down my uncle while some went and checked out his vehicle. When they finally let him through, I motioned for Joe to take Lyric inside. Without any fuss or questions, she turned around and went with him.

"What are you doing here? And how do you even know I'm here?" I came straight out and asked. If he was standing in front of me, there was a strong possibility my father was aware of my location.

"Relax, only I know. I wasn't sure at first but something told me to come here and check," he answered.

"But why? That's what I'm confused about," I retorted.

"What your father has done and doing, I do not condone. Yes, that's my brother, but you're my nephew and someone I hold dear to my heart. Not many people I feel like that about, and you know that."

I nodded because he was right. My uncle was very laid back and closed off. He stayed to himself but still handled business.

He was one of those quiet lethal muthafuckers you would have to worry about.

"Where this place you?" I wanted to know.

"I'm trying to stay out of it, but it's becoming hard. Listen, you need to call a truce with your father, come to some sort of agreement. You can't be running for the rest of your life or at least until he's dead or even you, for that matter."

"I'm not laying down Unc, fuck that!" I snapped, making people look my way.

"It's not laying down, it's being smart. Your father just wants the girl to return to her husband, right?" I nodded. "He didn't say shit about what happens after, correct?"

"Mmmhmmm."

"Take this from me, keep your friends close but your enemies closer." He tapped me on the shoulder and walked off.

With all that was said, he spoke with sincerity; I believed every word he was speaking. My mind started racing with ideas and all sorts of shit. I caught on to what Uncle Frank was trying to lay out. Although it made sense, I had to really sit on it and think things through. I wasn't the only person I had to worry about.

I watched him get back in his car and drive away, then made my way upstairs to a worried Lyric. As soon as I walked through the door, Lyric jumped off the couch and ran to me.

"Relax, baby, a nigga fine," I chuckled.

"I see that now." She rolled her eyes in sarcasm. "But for real, I need to talk to you."

"Aight, come on." I took her hand, led her to the bedroom and closed the door.

We sat at the foot of the bed side by side, as I held her hand in mine. "What's on your mind?" I asked her.

She took a minute to say anything; she just stared at the ground.

"I'm scared, Logan. I'm scared we won't make it out of all of this alive," she confessed. Hearing her words pained me; I never wanted her to feel fear in no sort of way. From the moment her file hit my hands, I just knew her life wouldn't have been the same. I just didn't know I would've been part of the reason why it wasn't.

"Lyric, on some real shit, I'm sorry you even have to go through this. From the start up until now, you don't deserve none of it," I stressed. "With my last dying breath, I will make sure you and our baby straight, that's a promise I will keep."

I knew she wanted things to end, shit, I did too. It was only a matter of time, and I believed that visit from my uncle and Lyric's feelings pushed me to want to figure things out sooner rather than later.

"Baby, my uncle gave me an idea, but it's only if you agree to it. If not, I'll find another way," I suggested.

"Wassup? Talk to me." She turned to face me fully with a curious look on her face.

"My father only doing all of this to get you back home to your husband. Once that happens, he's satisfied. What happens after isn't on him or his conscience, so he wouldn't care. What if I said I go speak to my Pops, make a truce with him, and let you go back home—"

"What?" she raised her voice.

"Hold on, can I finish?"

"Go ahead." She curled her lip.

"You go back home, so the deal between your husband and my Pops is fulfilled. You drain that fool of everything he got and then officially leave him. I know he won't lay down so easily, so I may have to make him." I looked at her reaction closely.

"You think that will work? I really don't want you to hurt him. I'll just do what I have to do and get a divorce, it was already in the works already," she informed me.

"Even better. You think you can handle it though?"

She looked at me in my eyes and held my hands. "Anything to be with you."

"Love you, baby girl."

"I love you more." She reached over and kissed me deeply.

After Lyric and I had our talk, we ordered something to eat and chilled for a bit. I massaged her hand and helped her out with her exercises, even though she didn't need me; it was just the thought that counted. Once she went down to rest for a little, I figured it was time I made the phone call to my father, do I did.

Ring! Ring!

The phone rang out and went to voicemail. Just when I thought about it probably not being the right time, he called back.

"Who is this?" he asked, as soon as I answered.

"It's Logan," I simply answered.

"Logan, well, hello Son," he said in a sarcastic tone.

"Don't son me," I shot.

"What did I do to deserve this call?"

"I want to have a sit down, figure things out," I offered. I didn't come right out and tell him my plan because I wanted him to feel like he was in control of everything and I was at his mercy. There wasn't just a plan in place for Lyric and her husband, there was one brewing for him as well.

"Oh, is that right? Tired of running, huh?" he gloated.

"You want to or not?"

"Sure, come by the house when you're ready."

"Better not be no funny shit either," I told him.

"It won't be, just come home."

I cringed at the word home because why the fuck did he feel the need to say that shit? It was nothing about that place I'd consider home or with him for a matter of fact.

Without saying another word, I just hung the phone up and saw the look on Joe's face. "You ready?" I asked him.

"I'm with whatever you on," he assured me.

The following morning as Lyric, Joe, and I headed outside to the truck, Tione and his guys were already outside waiting. I called him up the night before and told him of my plans.

"You don't miss a beat, my guy," I joked.

"Hell nah, my nigga." He dapped me up.

Joe placed our things inside the truck and got Lyric settled in while I chopped it up with Tione for a minute.

"This the last time I'm seeing you or what?" he came out and asked.

"Nah, it's actually not and trust me when I say that."

"My nigga." He pulled me in for a brotherly hug. "You call me the moment shit don't feel right. I'm forever ready."

"That's a fact, I got chu," I chuckled, but I knew he was dead ass serious. When I went to walk away and get in the vee, he stopped me one last time.

"Aye, make sure and give your girl and Joey my number!" he yelled out.

"My name is Joe," Joe corrected him with a straight face.

"Yeah, that's what I said," Tione laughed.

That fool was always on some funny shit, but he was my brother, nevertheless, so was Joe. I did listen to him and gave both Lyric and Joe his number, in case of anything.

When we hopped in the truck and pulled off, I just closed my eyes and spoke to the Lord the entire ride there. He was the only person who could've made sure shit didn't go south when we arrived.

As soon as we got to Staten Island, Joe went to a low-key hotel to drop Lyric off. I didn't feel comfortable taking her to the meeting. When things were sorted out and agreed upon, then I would've went back and got her. We made sure she was safe and had whatever it was she needed for the time being.

Once I felt she was straight, Joe and I hopped on the highway to my Pops' house.

About a half an hour later, we were pulling up to the gate of his mansion. When the guards saw us, you could tell they were tense and uneasy about our presence. I had to remember, between Joe and I, we did take out a handful of them from the night everything blew up in flames.

Without having to say a word to any of them, the gate opened and we were allowed access onto the premises. Joe drove the car to the front of the house, parked, and cut the engine. By that time, Phil had walked out the front door and was waiting for us at the top of the steps.

"You ready?" I asked Joe.

"Been ready, let's go."

We climbed out the car and made our way up the steps towards Phil, who wore a straight face, not showing any emotion.

"Logan," he stated and nodded his head in Joe's direction. "I'll need to search you before you can come in."

"Do you," I told him, then lifted my arms and opened them wide.

After he searched me, he searched Joe and told us to follow him. Walking through the house gave me an eerie feeling, but I just shook it off and continued to make my way to his office. When we finally reached it, Phil stepped aside to let me in but stopped Joe.

"Wait out here, let them speak alone," he told him.

Joe looked at me for approval, so I nodded my head, letting

him know it was okay. His old ass wasn't about that life anyway; I could've easily put him on his back if he even tried to act up.

When I walked into the office, my father was sitting at his desk waiting patiently for me to come in.

"Hello, Logan," he greeted nonchalantly.

"What's good, Pa?" I put emphasis on his name. "Please, have a seat." I motioned for me to sit down anywhere in the room.

I went ahead and found a spot on the couch, a good distance away from him. It took all the self-control I had to stay calm and not jump and drag his ass for everything he'd done.

"You okay there?" He pointed to my arm.

"Yeah, I'm good, ain't nothing but a little scratch." I smirked.

"Ahhh, I see."

"So, what's up? What you want from me, old man?"

"You know exactly what I want, the girl." He rocked back in his chair and clasped his hands together.

"Why? Why you want her so bad?"

"I told the man I would give him his wife back alive if he paid me what he owed. Well, he has paid up, well almost. He has the remainder of the money, but I wouldn't take his calls to receive it because I don't have what's his," he raised his voice.

"Lyric isn't his, she's mine," I corrected him.

He bussed out laughing hysterically. "Yours? Wow. You really fell for her," he said more as a statement than a question.

I stayed quiet and just looked at him.

"Okay, here's what we can do. Give the girl back in one piece; then, you kill him," he suggested with a shrug.

It was like he was in my head because that was going to be my plan from the jump. That was just to show how much we thought alike sometimes.

"So, once I let her go back, you don't care what I do afterwards?" I raised an eyebrow.

"Absolutely not, my involvement will be completely done," he assured me.

I believed him too; my father was always a man of his word. The main reason we were in the predicament we were in anyway was because he had to make sure he fulfilled his end of the deal.

"And things with us?" I had to ask.

"Water under the bridge." He smiled.

For you it is, not for me, I thought to myself.

"She'll be returned." I stood to my feet. "For now. So, go ahead and make the call for him to send you the rest of your cheddar."

I left the office with just a little weight lifted off my back. In a way, I was happy we came to an understanding for the most part. Things were getting hectic and it was affecting Lyric's mental, which I couldn't have with her condition.

Once the meeting was over, Joe and I got out of dodge and made our way back to Lyric. On our way there, we stopped, got some new iPhones and activated them. The moment Lyric was to leave my side, I needed to have constant contact with her.

The look on her face when we returned spoke a million words; she was extra happy as hell to see me.

"I'm so glad you made it back safe. That tells me everything went good?" she quizzed.

"Yeah, everything straight. I still feel uneasy letting you go back, but it's only for a little, aight?" I pulled her chin up with my index finger and pecked her lips.

Joe was waiting in the truck for us, so I quickly gathered her things from the room and got her to the vehicle. Once inside, she leaned against my good side and just closed her eyes. I knew she was mentally preparing herself to see him and just be back in that environment in general.

I wasn't trippin' not one bit I trusted Lyric and knew she'd hold shit down. Chadd wasn't the type of muthafucker I had to worry about either; he was soft and nowhere near a threat to me. Besides, we were back on the island and I'd only be one call away.

After what seemed to be the fastest drive ever, we pulled up to Lyric's house. She sat back and looked out the window, not moving an inch.

"Baby." I nudged her lightly.

"Huh? My bad, I just zoned out for a second," she stated the obvious.

"It's aight. You don't have to do this if you don't want to," I told her once again.

"No, I have to. It's the best way to handle everything. I got this." She squeezed my hand.

She grabbed her little bag with her books and stuff in it. I handed her the new phone and told her it was for an open line of communication.

"Let me get some lips." I turned her face towards me.

"Which ones?" she joked.

"Shit, I'll take both sets right now, don't tempt me."

She laughed and leaned in for a kiss. We locked lips for a while, as if it was going to be the last time we saw each other. Finally pulling away, she took a deep breath and let it out before opening the door and sliding out the truck. I watched her slowly put one foot in front the other, as she made her way up the driveway.

Chadd's car wasn't there, so I felt a little better that she'd have some time to wine down and get settled without him trying to be in her face. Lyric stopped at the door, entered a code to a security box and pulled out a pair of keys. She reluctantly pushed it into the keyhole, turned it, and opened the door. Before walking inside the house, she turned around and looked at the truck. She hung her head and went inside, shutting the door behind her.

CHAPTER 9

LYRIC

Stepping foot back into the place I supposedly called home gave me mixed feelings. While I was happy to be safe and in the comfort of my place, I was also down-hearted because I wasn't with Logan. As I made my way in further, I noticed how unkept the place was. It had a bad stench and looked horrible. I knew Chadd wasn't a cleaner, but it showed badly.

After fighting my way through the horrible smell, I finally reached the bedroom upstairs. When I walked in, the bed was neatly made and it seem as though nothing in the room had been touched for a while, especially my things. I wasn't sure if Chadd was even staying at the house or not because it sure didn't look like it.

I dropped my bag and phone on the bed and plopped down on it. While I wanted to spring into action and clean the place up, I decided to jump in the shower first. It wasn't no better feeling than bathing in your own bathroom.

When I went to start the shower, I noticed dust all over the place. More and more, I realized Chadd either didn't stay home or he just didn't use our room. I told myself I'd check the guest bedroom to see if it was the same as the rest of the house.

Stripping out of my clothes, I stepped into the shower and under the water. I wanted to wash my hair and groom myself properly but I knew I'd want to do all of that after I cleaned up. Making things quick, I soaped, rinsed, repeated three times, making sure to get all my creased, and got my ass out.

I looked at my phone and saw it was still early in the afternoon. We'd woken up early that morning around six o'clock to leave for Staten Island. I figured I had a good amount of time to get the place in some sort of order before Chadd returned home, unless Lo's father called him and told him I was already here, which I prayed he didn't.

Lo texted me and told me he and Joe were heading to his condo to settle in and figure some things out. I was happy he didn't go back to the mansion he shared with his wife, or at least not yet. We didn't get a chance to speak on their situation but I already knew it was a done deal, just like Chadd and I were.

I slipped on some house clothes and jumped right into cleaning. Of course, I took my time when things required both my hands. And when it came to chemicals, I didn't use too much of it; I could've heard Lo in my head cursing me out if I did. I thanked God I wasn't experiencing morning sickness because it would've held me back from getting the place together and, most importantly, it would've sold me out to Chadd.

Because I was a BBW and had a nice amount of meat on my bones, I didn't show. I was only in my first trimester anyway, so I knew I was going to be able to hide it for a while.

Three hours later, with an aching body and hand, the house was back in order and smelling like something. I was glad it was the spring time, so I was able to open up the windows and back door to let in some fresh air, that way I didn't suffocate myself with the cleaning supplies.

One of the first things I made sure to tackle was my tub, that was one of my favorite places to spend time and, after all that I'd been through and one hell of a cleaning spree, a nice hot bath was screaming my name.

I turned on my playlist from my laptop that was connected to my speakers and lit my Snuggly Sweater scented candle from Au'Shay Home while the tub filled up. I tossed a strawberry bath bomb from Bath and Body Works and watched it foam up in the water.

Taking my time, I stepped inside the tub and got comfortable. I rested my head back and closed my eyes, enjoying the hot water that was relaxing my muscles and body overall.

I stayed in the tub for a good while, just until the water started to become cold. Running in the shower, I rinsed off the soap studs and got right out. I handled my skin care, then went ahead and make sure everywhere was dry before applying lotion all over my body.

There were no plans to leave the house, even if Chadd tried. I figured ordering some food would've done just fine. So, I went ahead and put on some night clothes to feel comfortable and relaxed.

Once I was dressed, I ordered some food from one of my usual steak places and waited patiently for it to be delivered. While I waited, I jumped on my laptop and checked my email. I braced myself for a boatload of emails, text, and calls. My phone was synced to my MacBook, so everything was on there, even though I no longer had that phone. I lost it the night of the launch party when I was taken. I wasn't sure if it just dropped and was left there, or if Lo's father had it. Either way, it was gone and no longer in my possession. I was grateful I had every-thing on my laptop though.

There were so many concerning messages from my loved ones, from Lori-Ann to Nick and my mother, even Irene. The way I left that night, or at least that's what they thought, just seemed off and unusual about me, so I didn't blame everyone for being worried. I checked my social media and even fans were asking where I'd been. One thing about me, I was always active on my pages and always engaging with the readers.

Everyone knew shit was off, and that's when I realized I had to do damage control and turn into a PR rep for myself. There was no way I could've came out and told the truth about every-thing that happened. I had to make a story up, one that was believable.

Just when I started to become overwhelmed with everything, my phone started to ring as well as the doorbell.

"Hello?" I answered.

"Hi, I'm here with your food," the guy on the line said.

"I'm coming."

I hung up and made my way downstairs. By the time I reached the door, it was being opened for me by Chadd.

He looked like he saw a ghost mixed with excitement. He dropped his briefcase and pulled me into his arms, something that felt so off and weird. I couldn't remember the last time he hugged me with so much care and passion. Going along with things, I hugged him back tightly.

"Ahhh, so who's going to pay for the food?" the delivery guy blurted out and asked, causing us to break our embrace.

"Oh, here." Chadd went into his pocket, got his wallet, and paid the guy.

I took the food and went into the kitchen to dish it out. After all the cleaning I did, I was starving like I hadn't ate in days.

Chadd came into the kitchen and just stood there, staring at me. I stopped taking out the food and looked at him.

"What?" I asked.

"You're here, you're actually here." He had a little pitch in his voice.

He took a step closer to me, but I stepped back.

"I'm so sorry Lyric. I don't know what I'll have to do to get you to forgive me, but I'm willing to do anything," he pleaded with both hands in a praying position.

"Yeah? Well, it's going to be a whole lot you need to do," I said sternly. "While I'm happy to be home, I wish it wasn't here with you." I rolled my eyes, reverting my attention back to the food.

Being the woman I was, I still took his food out and placed it at his seat at the table. I guess it was the least I could've done, he did pay for the food.

I sat down and started to eat while he went and washed his hands and stuff before joining me at the table. We ate in silence, and I was grateful for it. If it was one thing about Chadd, he wasn't the confrontational type, so he'd watch what he say or didn't say anything at all until I started up a conversation.

When dinner was over, I put both our plates in the dishwasher and went upstairs to my room. I figured it was only my room since he was staying in the guest room while I was gone. While cleaning, I noticed the room being occupied, so I just put two and two together.

Before climbing into bed, I grabbed one of the books on the shelf under my *have to read* section. I cracked the baby open but, before I could read one word, Chadd appeared at the door.

"I know it's bad timing, but if and when you feel up to it, contact your sister and Nick. They filed a missing person's report and detectives came by asking questions the other day," he informed me.

"They did what?" My eyes damn near popped out of my head.

"Yeah, I mean, I couldn't fault them for it, but I'm just

grateful you came back before things got out of hand with the police."

"Right. Thanks, I'll reach out to them in a little bit. I know they'll want to come over tomorrow, so I'll make sure they do while you're at work."

"Sounds good. Alright, I know you had a long day. I see the house is back to its original state. I was too depressed and out of it mentally to even care to clean," he confessed.

"Yeah, you know I can't be in an unclean space. But, good-night," I told him and reopened the book.

He caught the hint and left the room. I started to read some more of the book but, before I got deep into it, I decided to send Lori-Ann and Nick a text.

> Me: Hey guys, it's me, Lyric. I know you've been bent out of shape worried about me, but I'm fine. I am back home so, if you can, come by tomorrow. Goodnight, love you.

After I hit the send button, I went ahead and got into read-ing, which I did for a good hour, then eventually fell asleep, a peaceful one at that..

THE NEXT MORNING, I WANTED TO SLEEP IN AND REST some more but, between my phone continuously pinging, the birds chirping, and hearing Chadd leaving out, I just got myself up. I knew Lori-Ann and Nick would've been at my door early on anyway, so I got myself together for their arrival.

I woke up to a text from my love, which allowed me to start my day off right.

> The King: Good morning, baby. I hope you slept well on your first night back. I know it ain't the same without me but shit gon change soon. Make sure you eat something good and do your exercises. Talk to you when you wake up. Love you.

His message was sent at like five o'clock in the morning. Logan was an early bird, went to bed late and woke up early. I wasn't sure how he did it, but he did.

I shot him back a good morning text, then went into the bathroom to brush my teeth, wash my face, and take a quick shower. As if it was perfect timing, when I got out the shower and got myself dressed, the doorbell was ringing. I went down-stairs to open the door and, of course, it was Lori-Ann and Nick.

The moment I unlocked the door, I didn't even have to pull it open; they both rushed in and stormed me.

"Lyric, oh, my God!" Nick squealed loudly.

"Thank God, you're okay," Lori-Ann exclaimed.

They both were hugging onto me, giving me damn near no room to breathe. Finally letting up, I looked at their faces and saw how much they loved me. You know they say you realized how much you're loved when something bad happens, even though they didn't know exactly what went on.

"I missed you guys so much." I held both their hands.

"Awwww, pooh," Nick cooed. "That's cool and all, bitch, you need to run us the tea because you had us thinking Chadd done did something to you."

"Yeah, about that." I turned around, walked into the living room and took a seat on the couch. When they sat down, I began to speak. "Before I say anything, y'all really filed a missing person's report?" I tilted my head to the side.

"Hell yeah, what you thought we was gon' do? Sit around and not get answers?" Nick jumped up and said.

"Shit, that reminds me." Lori started searching her phone and, next thing I knew, I heard a FaceTime call being made. "Good morning, Ms. Wright. I'm here with her now." She turned the camera towards me, and I saw a white woman on the screen.

"Hello, Mrs. Larson, good to see you made it back home safely. You had your family worried," the woman said.

"Thank you and, yeah, I just needed some time away. Everything's good over there though, thank you, again."

Lori-Ann took the camera off me and quickly wrapped up her conversation with who I assumed to be the detective that was handling my missing person's case.

"Okay, now that that's out the way, tea, now," Nick pressed.

I rolled my eyes playfully in annoyance. "I was away with Logan, we—"

"The same guy I had to tell you to go and get yours with?" Nick cut me off to ask.

"Yes, Nick," I giggled. "We had been seeing each other and, with a lot that was going on in both of our lives, we decided to go incognito. Sorry I alarmed y'all, but it just happened," I kind of sort of lied but told the truth too.

Yes, I was kidnapped against my own will but, after everything, I was where I wanted to be, with Lo.

"So, are you getting a divorce?" Lori questioned.

"Yes, I am," I announced.

"Bitch, even though you had me shook and worried, I'm for it and super happy for you," Nick beamed as he got up and came and gave me a hug.

"Yeah, if you're happy, then I'm happy," Lori added and joined in on the hug.

I wasn't truly ready yet to tell anyone I was pregnant. Honestly, I was still in disbelief and didn't want to jinx it. With PCOS, it was hard to get pregnant, but it was also hard to stay pregnant. So, when I felt the time was right, I would let everyone know. Plus, I was still married, and that could cause me to lose in a divorce battle if I wanted to drain Chadd dry.

All three of us just chilled, talked, and caught up with each other's lives; it was like I never left in the first place. It was a great feeling being back around my support system after going through all that I did. I felt some sort of peace, but I knew I'd feel whole when I was able to be with Logan without any restrictions.

CHAPTER 10

LOGAN

The morning after being back in Staten Island, I caught myself turning over trying to reach for Lyric. When I realized where I was and that I was alone, it only reminded me I had to get my woman back by my side.

I went straight to my condo after we dropped Lyric off at her house. Going to the mansion I shared with Cat wasn't the brightest idea for me at the moment, but I knew it had to happen. At the end of the day, that was my shit, that hoe ain't put nothing towards my spot. All she ever did was shop and spend my money and suck my father's dick.

Joe went to handle his personal affairs, leaving me to do my own thing. I knew I was good in the streets but I needed to start to build back up a team, a loyal one at that. For the time being, it was just Joe and I until I found some solid muthafuckers.

Still lying in the bed, I searched around for my phone. When I got it, I saw Lyric had texted me back from earlier. I barely slept the night we got back, and then I was up early as hell, so I shot her a text to wake up too. After I did my morning workout and ate, tiredness finally took over and I went to rest. I dialed my Uncle Frank number and pressed called.

"Hello?" he answered hesitantly.

"It's me Unc, Lo," I announced myself.

No one had my new number except for Lyric and Joe, so I expected him to answer the way he did.

"Oh, ok ok. What's going on kid?" he asked, sounding happy to hear from me.

"Nothing much, I'm back on the island. I want to see you."

"You know where to find me."

"Say less."

No more words needed to be spoken, so we just hung up. I rolled out of bed and went into the bathroom to brush my teeth and freshen up. Going through my closet, I picked out a fire fit just because I hadn't worn no drip in months. I was feeling like a straight up bum ass nigga.

With nowhere important to go, I still ended up throwing on a whole Amiri fit with some glossy Pradas on my feet. I placed my thick ass gold Cuban around my neck and wrist, along with my Rolex and diamond-filled ring. Looking in the mirror, I recognized that guy that was staring back at me and I didn't plan on losing sight of him again.

Because my favorite car, the Porsche, was wrecked, I had to jump in the only other vehicle I had at the condo, my Range Rover. All my other cars and shit was at the mansion, so I knew I'd be visiting there sooner rather than later.

I hopped in my truck and started it up. While I waited for it to run for a little while, I shot Joe a text, letting him know I was on my way to see my uncle and I was just checking in on things with him. When I sent the message, I reached over and checked my glove compartment to make sure my gun was inside. Once I located it, I put the truck in drive and was on my way.

About a half an hour later, I was pulling up to Uncle Frank's auto shop. I parked and climbed out the Range, bypassed all his workers and made my way inside. I knocked on the door and waited for him to answer.

"Who is it?" I heard him yell.

"Lo!"

"Come in."

When I walked into his office, he stood to his feet, walked around his desk, and came and hugged me.

"What's good, Unc?" I asked while in his embrace.

"I'm just happy to see your ass alive and well." He tapped my back mad hard.

"I'm good, man, I'm good."

We broke our embrace and took a seat on his office couch.

"So, I'm guessing you figured out what I was trying to tell you, and you took my advice, eh?" he smirked.

"Yeah, I must admit, I did. At first, I wasn't trying to hear it; I didn't want to think about fixing shit with my Pops. He violated in the worst way. But, after you left, Lyric got in my ear and my heart, so I had to reconsider, for her sake," I confessed.

"And I'm happy you did. You're a stubborn ass kid but a very wise one."

Although I was thirty-two years old, my uncle stayed calling me kid. It had been his thing since I was a baby and only he was allowed to call me that.

"Thanks Unc."

"Now, what's about to happen with you and that wife of yours?" He raised a brow.

"Man, fuck that bitch. I'm divorcing her, no questions asked. Before all the shit happened, I wasn't in love with her anyway, so I just need to break all ties with her. I have a woman, one I'd like to have my last name and build a family with."

"Lyric." He smiled.

"Yeah." I smiled too; I couldn't hold it back.

Just speaking of her or thinking about her, I would catch myself smiling or in a good mood; she just had that effect on a nigga.

"If she makes you happy, go for it. You know I'll be here to support you."

I nodded in acknowledgment.

"Just make sure you do things right when it's time to clean up the mess," he advised.

"I got chu."

We spoke for about another hour or so. He was always the one dropping gems and the whole nine on me. I appreciated the relationship my uncle and I had. We had a stronger bond than me and my father did, even before I found out about his betrayal.

When I was leaving the shop, Lyric shot me a text that made me feel softer than a baby's bottom.

> Queen: I think I felt some flutters, or I may be tripping. But it's happening off and on.

> Me: I'm booking you a doctor's appointment right now.

> Queen: Okay. (Heart emoji).

Before I even pulled off, I got on the phone with my usual doctor I had. He had an OBGYN partner, which was his wife at the same office Cat would go and see.

"Doctor Rice speaking, how may I help you?" he answered.

"Doc, it's Logan Luchiano," I announced.

"Hey, Logan, how are you? Everything good?"

"Yeah, yeah. I was calling to set up an appointment to see your wife. I just found out I'm expecting and need to have her checked out," I informed him.

"Oh, congratulations to you and your wife."

"No, it's not her, unfortunately, we're no longer together. It's my girlfriend that's pregnant," I corrected him. I didn't feel not one ounce of guilt for telling him that either; it was the truth.

"Okay, I see. Congratulations to you both. I see my wife has an opening for tomorrow morning at nine, how's that?"

"Perfect, we'll see you guys then."

"Alright, have a great rest of your day, Logan."

"You too, doc."

As soon as I hung up, I texted Lyric.

Me: Doctor's appointment tomorrow for nine a.m., so be ready.

Queen: Damn, that was fast as hell. You wasn't playing but, okay, I will be, baby. Thanks!

I was excited about the appointment, and I knew since I was going there, I'd have to see Doctor Rice about my gunshot wound, just to make sure it was healing properly. That's when I realized I'd have to go to the house to grab my medical card and documents I always took to my visits.

Dreading going there so soon, I figured I might as well get it out the way; I honestly prayed she wasn't home when I arrived.

As I was inching towards the house, a flashback of the accident hit me. I looked at the very spot we were hit before being turned over a few times, and a wicked feeling came over me.

Shaking it off, I continued to the gate, which was closed of course, but there was a guard at his post. I was happy to see some of them were still working and making sure my shit was safe.

"Boss, you're back," the guy at the gate exclaimed.

I barely knew any of their names; I just knew them by face. Getting personal wasn't my thing; the only person that was able to get in was Joe, and that was because we grew up together and he was my head of security.

The gate opened and I pulled onto the compound, wrapping around the roundabout in from the house. I didn't see Cat's car parked out front, so I figured she was out, which was a good thing. I hurriedly got out the car and ran up to the front door.

Using my key felt weird, but I opened the door and entered. The place was quiet but, a few moments later, Luci appeared in the hall.

"Señor, Hola!" Her face lit up.

"Hi, Luci. How are you?" I went and gave her a quick hug.

"Good, good, I'm so happy to see you."

"Thank you. Where's Cat?" I asked, not trying to beat around the bush.

"She went out somewhere." She shrugged.

"Okay, thank you."

"Si, señor."

I went into my man cave and headed straight for my safe. Inside, I grabbed my medical folder that contained everything I needed. Knowing I needed a few more things, I swiftly moved about the house to grab up what I could for the time being.

The first stop I made was my bedroom. I got a suitcase and laid it on the bed. Browsing through my closet, I took a couple of clothing items, sneakers, and other things and dumped it in the suitcase.

Making my way back downstairs, it was just my luck Cat walked in the front door.

Fuck, I thought I had a clean get away, I cursed myself.

"Logan," Cat said in disbelief.

Ignoring her presence, I continued down the stairs and walked past her. I rested the suitcase near the door and went ahead to the garage. I heard her footsteps following me, but I didn't even look back.

"Logan, please say something," she whined.

I didn't know what the fuck she wanted me to say. If anything, she was the one who had some explaining to do. At that point, I didn't even want to hear anything from her because overall, I didn't care.

Going through the key box, I looked for the key to my Bentley. As soon as I found it, I turned and walked right pass her once again and back into the house. I said bye to Luci and made my way to the front. As I picked up the suitcase, ready to head out the door, Cat came flying pass, closing the door shut and standing in front of it.

"Come on, man, let me leave. I don't have time for this shit," I spat.

"Logan, I'm so sorry, please let me explain. It's not what you think," she cried.

Not one drop of tear moved me. I was officially over Catteleya and it was no turning back, no matter what.

"Listen, I'm trying my best not to hurt your feelings, just let me be. It's done and over with. There's no more us, so there's no need of you to explain."

"But I want to, you deserve an explanation. Please, I hate myself for everything that happen."

"It's cool, Cat." I smirked. "Just let me leave."

I gently pushed pass her and got to open the door, but I had one more thing to say before I left out. "Expect some papers to sign. They'll be arriving soon."

I turned and left without thinking twice about her feelings. No one cared about me when they were doing their bullshit.

Fuck her, disrespectfully.

CHAPTER 11

LYRIC

The moment I sent Lo a text about feeling something in my stomach, the man went straight into daddy mode and booked a doctor's appointment. I couldn't lie, it made me feel so good and secured that he was on it and excited about the baby. Most men probably would've been hesitant about it; I mean, we were only starting to build our relationship for real.

One he told me the time of the appointment, I was happy because Chadd was going to be at work, and I wouldn't have to explain myself to him. He'd been keeping his distance, giving me space in the house. Surprisingly, he even came home right after work the day after I came back. I didn't know the status of him and Kayla's situation since I'd been gone, but I knew eventually I would've found out.

The morning of the appointment, I woke up early enough to get myself together. Logan was up at the crack of dawn already, patiently waiting for me to open my eyes. As soon as I popped up, the first thing I did was reach for my phone. It was something about getting a good morning text from the one you loved the most.

> The King: Get yo ass up and hurry up and meet me

> The King: Oh yeah, good morning, hope you and my son slept well

What the hell, I thought to myself as I laughed. *This man a whole mess.*

> Me: Good morning, baby. I'm up and getting ready, sheesh. (Heart emoji)

I couldn't wait to see Lo so, the faster I got ready, the quicker I got to be in his arms. The whole being away from each other thing was hard and gave me more of a reason to have to go revisit the lawyer again to put things back into motion.

Within an hour of waking up, I handled my hygiene, drank some tea, since I wasn't in the mood to eat breakfast, and was dressed and ready to go. It was the first time I was about to leave the house and go out and about on my own. My car was parked inside the garage, which I figured was where it stayed the entire time. I went in there and started it, allowing it to run for a few minutes since it wasn't being used for a few months.

I made sure the house was locked and secured, then made my way back to the garage. I hopped in, backed out and went about my way to the address Logan told me to meet him at.

The morning traffic had already died down; plus, it was mostly always hectic going towards the city. Where I was headed was the opposite direction. About a half an hour later, the GPS told me I had arrived at my destination. I looked around and saw the doctor's office. Pulling into the parking lot, I found a parking spot and called Lo to see where he was.

Ring! Ring! Ring!

"You look even more beautiful than before," he stated as soon as he answered the phone.

"What? Where are you?" I giggled and started looking around.

"Right across from you, sitting in the black Bentley."

Squinting my eyes to see, I saw the very car he was talking about. "Bye, Lo." I hung up and got out my car, as he did the same. "Oh, you fancy, fancy, huh?" I nodded towards his vehicle.

"Man, that ain't shit." He waved me off as he walked towards me with open arms.

I walked right into his sweet scent and held onto him tightly, feeling his tight muscles. "I missed you so much," I whispered loud enough for him to hear.

"Miss you too, shorty." He kissed my forehead. "Come on, let's go check on my son."

"You so hell bent on it being a boy; what if it's a girl?" I popped my neck at him.

"I know it's a boy and, if it do turn out to be a girl, which I know it won't, that's gon' be my princess." He shrugged.

I was just totally in love with his energy. We walked inside the doctor's office hand in hand, as if we were a long-time couple madly in love.

"Good morning, how may I help you?" a young lady at the desk asked.

"Luchiano for Doctor Rice," Lo stated.

"Yes, she's expecting you all. Right this way." She motioned for us to follow her to the back.

We entered an empty examination room and was told to hold tight. Not even a few minutes later, an older black woman who I assumed to be Doctor Rice came in.

"Hello, good morning. I'm Doctor Rice," she introduced herself to me with a warm handshake. "How are you, Logan?" she turned and acknowledged him.

"I'm fine, doc. I hope all is well with you, the family, and business," he told her.

"Yes, it is. But I hear we have way more important news to discuss. You're going to be a father, congratulations." She smiled brightly. "Is this your first child as well?" she turned and asked me.

"Yes ma'am," I answered.

"Wonderful. Well, let's get down to business." She took a seat at the desk.

Doctor Rice had me fill out some paperwork asking questions

about my medical history of course and took some blood and urine samples from me. Logan sat there, looked, and listened to everything. He was just waiting patiently for her to do the ultrasound.

When we finished everything we needed to do, it was time to see the little miracle that was baking in my oven.

"Alright, I need you to lay back on the bed, lift your shirt up, and relax," Doctor Rice instructed.

Logan helped me get comfortable, then stood right by my side, holding my hand.

After entering my info into the machine, she squeezed the jelly-like substance onto my stomach and the probe. "You guys ready?" she asked with a smile.

We both looked at one another and nodded our heads. She placed the probe to my stomach. On the screen, we saw some action, but it was a little too much action.

"Ummm, why does it look like two babies?" I asked, confused.

"That's because it is," she confirmed. "Congratulations, you're having twins."

"What?" Logan raised his voice in excitement. "You sure that ain't a glitch or something shit?"

I slapped his hand because he cursed.

"Oh, my fault. Y'all know what I mean."

We all bussed out laughing.

"Nope, this is right. It's two little babies in there."

"Wow, just when I thought I couldn't even get pregnant, now I'm being blessed with two." I started to cry.

Logan hugged me to the best of his abilities since I was still lying on the bed. Doctor Rice was still conducting her imaging of the babies, making sure everything looked normal.

"You're just about eleven weeks pregnant, almost out of your first trimester," she informed us. "Have you been experiencing any morning sickness?"

"No, not really. I'd feel a little sick here and there but nothing major. No throwing up or any of that."

"You're one of the lucky ones. You seem to be having a pretty healthy pregnancy so far, and let's keep it that way. Get lots of rest, drink a lot of fluids, and please eat healthy. It's super easy to become a diabetic during your pregnancy, even though it's only temporary," she explained.

"Don't worry doc, I'm on her ass," Logan exclaimed.

I slapped his arm again, making everyone laugh. As we were wrapping up the appointment, another doctor came into the room to see Logan.

"Doctor Rice, what's good?" Logan greeted him.

Putting two and two together, the two doctors were either siblings or husband and wife.

"This must be the lucky lady, congratulations," he stated.

"Thank you."

He and Logan started to talk concerning his bullet wound, making us switch places. Logan sat on the bed while he took a look at it, and I sat on the chair.

"Whoever got it out and patched you did a good job; it's healing well," he told him.

"Alright, good. That's all I needed to know." He bobbed his head up and down like he was listening to music.

"Ms. Larson, I will be seeing you in another month, alright? But if anything happens between then or you feel a certain way, please call me," Doctor Rice told me, concluding our session.

Both Logan and I got our appointment dates for the next time around and headed out.

"You tryna go grab something to eat?" he asked me, as we walked back to our cars.

"Yeah, I haven't ate anything yet, just had some tea."

"Aye, we not finna be on that type of timing. You eating for three now, so act like it," he told me sternly.

"Yes Sir," I laughed, making him crack a smile.

"Follow me, I know a spot."

I jumped in the car and followed him out the parking lot and onto the streets.

Only ten minutes had passed, and we had arrived at a place that looked like a hole in a wall restaurant. I tried not to judge because one thing I knew for sure, Lo didn't eat at no bum ass place. It had to have some good food or something.

We parked up and went inside. It had a homey feel to it. The place resembled a house, like someone's grandmother or aunt's house.

"What's this place?" I asked, as we got seated.

"The best soul food spot you'll ever eat in your life," he exclaimed.

"The best? Well, okay then, let's see."

We ordered our food and drinks and, without having to

wait very long, it was out and in front of us. Holding hands, we said grace and immediately dug into our plates.

"Oh, this is good," I agreed after taking a good bite of my fried chicken.

I went ahead and tasted the candied yams and collard greens; both tasted delightful. Not to mention, the mac n cheese, the whole meal was the bomb, even this corn bread. Logan definitely knew places.

As we were eating, my phone vibrated so I took a peek at it to see who it was.

Chadd: Hey, would you be up for going out to dinner tonight? It's a business dinner and the potential client would love for me to bring you

Reading his message made me cringe. Instead of trying to invite me to a one-on-one dinner with just us to air some things out, his head was focused on business. I guess some people would never learn their lesson.

"What's wrong?" Lo asked, catching on to the change of my mood.

I showed him my phone, so he could read the message. All he did was chuckle and shake his head. "I'm about to tell him no," I insisted.

"Nah, go to the dinner, feel him out, and see where his head at. Observe his actions," he suggested.

"You think I should?"

"Yeah, go ahead. You know I ain't trippin'."

"Okay, I guess."

We continued to eat, but the vibe was a little off. I wasn't sure if it was me or if it was him. But that text just blew mine overall and, deep down inside, I knew it did to Lo as well.

Once we finished our meal, I started to feel tired, so we thought me going home was the best thing. I didn't want to leave him and, while I had thoughts of just going by him to rest, I knew it was too soon and had to keep up the show.

We parted ways and, as soon as I got home, I stripped out my clothes and jumped right into bed. I was out within a few minutes of my head hitting the pillow.

"Lyric, Lyric," I heard someone calling me. At first, I thought I was still dreaming but, when I felt a hand on my shoulder, I jumped up to see Chadd.

"Hey, did you get my text about tonight?" he asked.

"You woke me up to ask me about a text message?" I snapped with irritation in my voice.

"Sorry, but it's kind of a big deal. If you don't want to though, it's fine; I understand." He started to walk out the bedroom.

"I'll go. What time do I have to be ready for?" I gave him attitude.

"Be ready for seven."

"Cool."

I looked at my phone and saw it was five-thirty-five p.m.

Knowing me, when it came to stepping all the way out, which was required for a business dinner, I knew I had to get a head start on getting ready.

Before I got in the shower, I found something to wear. Lying out everything from my outfit to my make-up and things to do my hair with, I sprang into action and got myself dolled up. When the clock struck seven o'clock, I was walking down the stairs to leave.

"Wow, you look amazing," Chadd complimented, and it actually sounded sincere.

He held his arm out for me to latch onto. Reluctantly, I took it and went along with the flow. Bad as it was, I was forcing myself to go out that night, so I tried my best to not make it feel weird or have any tension between us.

When we arrived at the restaurant, the couple we were meeting was already there, along with John and his wife. An introduction was made, as well as a quick reconnection between John and his wife.

The whole time they spoke about investments and politics, two of which I didn't care for or had opinions on. I stayed quiet and just nodded my head when Chadd said something and looked pretty. I sat through one too many of these business dinners to know they didn't care to hear what I thought; they just wanted to see that Chadd was a family man.

When the night was over, everyone left, but Chadd and I stayed back. He requested we had some alone time, and I just agreed to it.

"How are you doing?" he solemnly asked.

"I'm doing okay, taking things one day at a time," I confessed.

"I see you're always moving your right hand. Something happened to it?"

"Ummm, yeah. I fell on it and broke it. Just trying to do some exercises to get it back to where it once was or at least close to it."

Chadd was not aware of everything that happened. All he knew was I was captured and held hostage. He didn't know about me running off with Logan, the accident, any of it.

"Got it. I'm really sorry you had to go through whatever it was you did without me. I should have been in your place."

You damn fucking right, I thought.

"We can't cry over spilt milk, right?"

"No, but I really want to make things right. Which is why I need to speak to you. There's some things I need to tell you." He sat up in his seat.

"Okay, speak, what's going on?" I raised an eyebrow.

"Lyric, I've been seeing Kayla," he blurted out.

I stayed quiet to act like I didn't know the news he was relaying.

"But that's not all of it, she's pregnant," he added.

Oh, I didn't know that part of it, I said to myself.

I was no longer acting and was very much shocked at the revelation. "She's what?" I asked, squinting my eyes at him.

"I'm sorry. I know I keep saying that for everything, but I truly am. We started messing around and, after you got taken, I started feeling so guilty and knew that I loved you with everything in me. You are who I'm meant to be with. I messed up, Lyric." He hung his head in defeat.

I still wasn't able to say a word. I just sat there looking clueless at that point.

"Like I said, I'm willing to do anything to make things right. I cut things off with Kayla and only speak to her if it has anything to do with the baby. I will be replacing her at the office as well. Baby, you can have access to everything of mine, whatever is it to regain my trust. My phone passcode, computer password, have access to all my accounts, everything," he rattled on.

"It's going to take everything in this world to make things right, Chadd," I told him.

"And I'm ready to give you it all."

CHAPTER 12

KAYLA

Ever since Lyric came back home, I'd been getting completely ignored. I mean, right before then, things were changing between Chadd and me. He barely spoke to me, only if it came to work related stuff at the office and about the baby outside of work. But things became worse once Lyric was back in the picture.

When Chadd and I started messing around, it was clear that he wasn't in love with her anymore, or at least that was what he used to say, along with his actions. We agreed to build something serious between us as things went on. He had planned on leaving her for me but, out of nowhere, he started acting different and being more and more distant.

While I had my own reasoning for doing things, I started to

fall for Chadd. It was one of the reasons Kevin couldn't stand the fact I was still dealing with him. He was able to tell that I started taking things personal, and I was.

I still wasn't sure if the baby was Chadd's or if it was Kevin's and, until I knew for sure which was the father, I needed to keep them both happy in some kind of way. Juggling both was becoming hard, well mostly on Kevin's end because he knew about Chadd while Chadd had no knowledge of him. The only thing was, both men thought the kid was theirs so, in Kevin's eyes, I was pregnant with his child and still hoeing around with my trick.

While at work, I overheard a few people speaking about a big business dinner between a potential client and Chadd. Continuing to eavesdrop, I heard he was taking his wife, so was John. Jealousy crept into me knowing she was just gone and came back into the mix of things like nothing happened.

I didn't tell Chadd, but there were nights I got on my knees and prayed she didn't return. If she did come back, I prayed she didn't want to have nothing to do with Chadd due to his self-ishness and carelessness. Clearly, God didn't hear my prayer or didn't find it worthy enough.

When she first returned, Chadd told me right away. He even mentioned to me that he was going to come clean about us and about the baby. At that moment, I wasn't sure what his motive was and what he had planned but, if he wanted to tell her, that was on him. I just hoped she didn't try to come and pull up on me because pregnant or not, I was going to be ready for whatever.

My phone chimed, snapping me out of my thoughts. The ringtone indicated it was an email. I went in, checked it and saw it was my co-payment bill from the doctor's office. Chadd handled all my medical bills and anything else pertaining to the baby, so I called him.

Ring! Ring! Ring!

The phone rang out and went to voicemail. I tried about three more times and got the same results, so I decided to screenshot the email and send it to her in a text message.

> Me: (Screenshot of email)

> Me: I'm not sure why it's so hard for me to get in contact with you now. You moving real weird, real funny acting. Okay!

Just when I sent the message, in walked Kevin from outside. I was on the living room couch just lying there watching TV.

"Wassup?" he greeted.

"Hi," I said nonchalantly; I wasn't in the mood.

"The fuck is wrong with you?" he asked, scrunching up his face.

"Nothing, Kevin. Why something gotta be wrong with me?"

"Bro, your whole demeanor gave it away. You got an attitude, the way you answered me and all like I did something to you."

I waved him off and continued to watch the TV.

"You lucky yo ass I pregnant. Keep playing with me, Kayla. I ain't that white nigga," he spat.

"What the fuck is that supposed to mean?" I jumped up because now, he had me fucked up.

Kevin was jealous of Chadd the moment he found out about him. Every change he got, he would fire shots his way. The sad part about it all was Chadd didn't even know his clown ass existed.

"Exactly what I said. Check yo self before I have to do it." He glared at me.

"Nigga, you bugging. Better go about your way, real shit."

He leaped from where he stood by the door all the way across the living room and grabbed me by the throat.

"Bitch, didn't I tell you to stop playing with me? Time and time again, I let you slide with disrespecting me. I don't give a fuck what your trick let you do, but I ain't him. I'll murk yo ass before you can even blink," he threatened.

He squeezed my throat a little tighter before letting go. I was seconds away from blacking out; I felt my soul leaving my body as my air supply was cut off. Tears flowed heavily down my cheeks as I gasped for air. Breathing in and out fast as hell, I tried to get my breathing under control. Once I felt it was leveling, I took deep breaths in and out.

Kevin stood over me the entire time, staring at me. He had this menacing expression on his face like he was ready to kill something or someone. I knew of his track record when it came to the streets. While he wasn't making that much money at the moment, he used to be the man in the streets. One reason many people feared him was because he was known to put down his murder game and didn't think twice about it.

"Ke-Kevin, why would you do that?" I cried.

He never choked me out that way before. Sometimes, when he got upset and we fell out, he'd just grab me up, but never hit me or try to damn near kill me. I knew, at that point, he was definitely feeling some kind of way about my situation and me altogether. I told myself I had to get away from him before things got worse, especially if it turned out that the baby wasn't his and it was Chadd's.

"Because I'm tired of your shit. Ever since you started dealing with that man, you changed. Like I wasn't the one taking care of you, making sure you was straight. All of a sudden, a nigga ain't good enough for you. Bro, you're pregnant with my child and still running down this nigga. Make it make sense."

"I told you I was just trying to get as much out of him as I can, that's all," I pleaded.

"Fuck that, I don't want you to see him no more. Cut all communication and all that. Should feel ashamed of yourself. A woman helped you get on your feet with a better job, and you turned around and fucked her husband." He shook his head.

But you wasn't saying that shit when I started bringing home that extra money, I said in my head. I wouldn't have dare spoken that out loud. The manner he was in, I would've probably been meeting my maker that night.

"Okay, I hear you."

"Find another job, Kayla. Shit is done and over with. If I

find out you still fucking with that clear muthafucker, I'll make sure you and him go six feet deep, you hear me?" he threatened.

For the first time in my life, I was scared. I knew good and well Kevin would live up to this threats, they were more so promises. I had to figure out a way to hurry up and find out if the baby was his or Chadd's, that way I could make a decision on how to move forward.

Fuck my life.

CHAPTER 13

LYRIC

It was pushing elevon o'clock at night when my craving started. I tried to ignore it and go back to sleep, but it just didn't go away. I slipped out of bed and went downstairs to the kitchen to see what I had that could curve it. Going through my snack cabinet, I saw not one thing that would satisfy me.

Chadd was asleep and, even if he was awake, I wouldn't have asked him to go and get shit for me. I ran back upstairs and texted Lo to let him know I was about to make a late-night store run.

> Me: Baby, I'm having wild cravings for chocolate and it's none here. I'm about to go to the nearby Rite Aid.

Almost immediately, he responded.

> The King: You're not about to leave out the house this time of night alone. Wait about ten minutes, I'm sending Joe.

I knew he wouldn't have liked the idea of me trying to go out that late by myself. For a minute, I thought he was going to come his damn self, but it was best he stayed his distance from the house, especially with the nosy ass neighbors we had.

While I waited for Joe to arrive, I went and got dressed, throwing on a comfortable sweatsuit. It wasn't even ten minutes, and Lo was texting me telling me to go outside.

I jumped off the bed, grabbed my wallet, and jetted down the stairs. Making minimal noise, I moved around with ease but quickly. I didn't want to wake Chadd and he start asking questions.

Once outside, I saw an SUV parked out front. Joe rolled down the window to show his face and put it back up. I observed my environment and swiftly made my way to the SUV.

"Hey, Joe," I sang as I got in the back.

"What's going on, Lyric?" he greeted.

"You got here fast as hell."

"I was in the area. Once Lo called, I came straight here."

"Oh, okay, makes sense." I shrugged. I sat back and enjoyed the ride. All I could've thought about was devouring some Snickers or Twix.

The ride to Rite Aid was short; it wasn't far and, of course, it was barely any cars on the streets. He parked near the entrance, so the walk wasn't a long one for me. I climbed out and went inside, happier than a kid in a candy store.

I went straight for the snack and candy section. Picking up a bunch of chocolate, I realized I wanted some other things. I started grabbing up some chips, cakes, and whatever else my eyes landed on. If I was able to, I would've bought the whole snack section. Once my arms were filled and I couldn't pick anything else up, I turned and started to make my way to the cash register.

On my way out the aisle, I overheard a guy on the phone; he was pretty upset.

"Yeah man, this bitch Kayla a trip. I don't know what else to do with her. One thing I know for sure, that Chadd mutha-fucker better count his days if he don't stay away," he spoke into the phone.

Chadd? Kayla? My eyebrows raised.

I went towards the voice and finally located him in the back by the freezer getting a drink out the fridge.

"Hi," I spoke in a moderate tone.

"Yo, let me call you right back, bro." He hung up the phone and turned his attention to me. "You look hella familiar," he stated.

"I kind of overheard you talking about Kayla and Chadd," I said hesitantly.

"So? I don't think that's your business."

"Actually, I think it is. If we're speaking of the same Kayla and Chadd, I'm Chadd's wife," I let it be known.

"Shit, now, I know who you are. I knew you looked familiar. I saw a few of your pictures when you just started fucking with Kayla trifling ass."

"Oh, I see. So, what have you all hyped up and upset, if you don't mind me asking? Wait, who are you to Kayla?" I went in for the kill.

"I'm her nigga, been that since we were kids. Your husband came throwing around money and she somehow convinced me to allow her to milk the nigga of his bread. Now, she pregnant with my seed and I want her to stay the fuck away from him and vice versa."

I wore a surprised expression on my face because I didn't want to give it away that I already knew about the affair. "She's pregnant? Are you sure it's yours if she been fucking my husband?" I speculated.

He got quiet; the question I asked definitely had the wheels in his head turning.

"You know, I never thought of that. I mean, she always said it was mine, so I just went with it. But, now that you mentioned it, who the fuck is the father?" he asked hypothetically.

"That's an excellent question. Now, if my husband thinks it's his, well, that is if he even knows. I think you need to have her get a DNA test done, as soon as possible," I suggested.

I could care less about their drama, but it would be wrong that Chadd thought it was his child when it wasn't.

"How though? She's still pregnant."

"There's a way," I assured him.

"Listen, I'm sorry all this shit happening to you and you had to find out this way, but thanks for the advice. I hope shit works out on your end," he said before walking off quickly.

I already knew love and I'm not the one who's going to be sorry, I thought.

THE NEXT MORNING, I WOKE UP WITH ONE MISSION and one mission only on my mind, to see the lawyer. With everything just unraveling about Chadd's affair, it was safe to say I would definitely win the divorce, even if it went to court. When I was finished with his ass, he would've wished he fucked over a stupid bitch and not a smart one like me.

I got up and did my normal morning routine: check my phone, respond to Lo and whoever else contacted me, get me a cup of tea, and handle my hygiene. I got dressed quickly and headed out the door. Mrs. Daniels' office was the destination and, even though she didn't know I was coming, I prayed she had an opening to see me.

When I arrived at her office, I went inside and saw there wasn't anyone in the waiting area, which a good sign for me.

"Good morning, welcome to Daniels' Law, how can we assist?" the receptionist greeted me.

"Hi, I'm Lyric—"

"Larson," I heard a voice say my last name.

I turned around and saw it was Mrs. Daniels herself standing there.

"It's fine, Lisa, let her through," she stated. "Come on, Lyric." She walked into her office with me in toe.

I didn't even get a chance to put my ass on a seat before she started shooting questions my way.

"Where have you been? You just disappeared on me. Did you get cold feet and changed your mind?" she asked.

"If only I could tell you but, no, I still want to move forward with the divorce. His mistress is pregnant and he actually came clean and told me everything. He's offered to give me full access to his accounts; he wants to do everything in his power to make things up to me," I informed her all at once.

"Whew, wow, ummm, okay then."

We both laughed out loud.

"I still have everything here ready for you to sign your name. Of course, with the new evidence, it makes your case an open and shut one. Say the word and I will file the paperwork with the courts, and he'll be served his papers less than a month."

"Do it," I simply said.

"It's done."

CHAPTER 14

CATTELEYA

A *divorce?* I was raised to not believe in that word. The family I was from didn't allow those to happen, no matter how tough it got. My mama and papa were married until my mama passed away. I just knew if Logan really did fall through with his threats, my family would definitely disown me.

After the night of the incident where Lorenzo and my secret got out, my father shut me out completely. I had not spoken to him and, when I did try to reach out, he didn't answer. I even went all the way to Mexico to see him, but they denied me entry to my own home.

I sunk into a bad depression. I had nobody to turn too, well, except for Sofia. The real meaningful people in my life didn't want nothing to do with me. Lorenzo wasn't my top favorite at the time but he didn't even want to see or speak to me. I had no father, no husband, no support system, just Luci to cook and clean for me.

In the morning time, I would usually get up early, workout and get my day started. That all went out the window when I felt I had nothing to live for. Luci would bring my breakfast to me in bed, along with the other meals throughout the day. The only time I went outside was for important reasons like doctors' visits or even the grocery with Luci just to get some air, only because she would force me.

I fucked up big time, and I knew it. Every day I prayed to God to give me another chance, but I guess he felt he gave me enough, so did Logan. In a way, I couldn't blame him for how he felt and wanting a divorce, but I wouldn't lie and say I was going to just sit back and allow him to leave me so easily, especially for another bitch.

When I returned home that night of the big fall out, I saw the wreck that was outside our gate. His Porsche was tore up but, when I didn't see him, I knew he got away. After checking the camera, I saw Joe helped him and that fat bitch flee.

My woman intuition told me it was more than he said was going on between and that chick that was being held in our basement. The way he looked at her and treated her told me more than I needed to know. Once I found out he fucked her, well, that's when it sealed the deal and confirmed my suspicion.

Knock! Knock!

"Yes, Luci," I answered from the bed.

I knew it was her because she was the only one here that moved about freely, besides the guards.

"Señor is here," she whispered.

I jumped out the bed wide eyed. It could've been only a second he was in the house, I wanted to lay my eyes on him and plead my case until I couldn't anymore.

"Where is he?"

"His room," she said, referring to his man cave.

"Gracias, Mami," I told her and slipped on the sweatpants I had on the lounge chair.

Running down the stairs, I quickly made my way to his man cave. When I got there, the door was closed shut. I contemplated whether to knock or just storm in because at that point, it wouldn't have matter either way; he was already in a sour mood with me.

Against my better judgement, I walked in without knocking, but I did so in a calm and not feisty manner. "Hi, Logan," I spoke up.

He was at the bar taking a sip of a drink and reading a paper. Although I spoke loud enough, he acted like he didn't hear me, so I walked in further and stood behind him.

"Bro, why are you so close to me?" he questioned with annoyance in his tone.

"Now, I'm your bro?"

He looked at me out of the corner of his eye. "What do you want, Cat?"

"You," I said softly.

"You can't have that."

"But why Logan? We're fuckin' married, not boyfriend and girlfriend, married. Til' death do us apart, remember!" I screamed and put my ring in his face.

"Won't be for long," he stated nonchalantly. He handed me a piece of paper and finally turned around, leaning up against the bar. "See, I had my lawyer draw that up. Remember, you signed a prenup, so you don't get shit. You sign that; it'll have the whole process go smooth once the official papers come back from the courts. That states you object to nothing and will get nothing when it's all said and done."

"What? Fuck outta here. Where am I supposed to go? What am I supposed to do?" I cried.

"I don't know, and I really don't give a fuck. Sign the paper, so I can be on my way. I got shit to do."

"Fuck you and your paper!" I threw it in his face.

Logan didn't even flinch. He just simply finished his drink, grabbed his phone and keys, and left out the room. I followed him all the way out the door, still cursing his ass out. When I saw him get in his car and started to drive out, I went and grabbed my keys. I was going to follow his ass to wherever was more important for him to be.

Quickly hopping in my car, I sped off the compound and went in the direction I saw him turn. I kept my distance though; I didn't want him to notice me trailing him. He was swerving in and out of lanes, making it easy for me to see him.

After following him for about fifteen minutes, he pulled into a shopping plaza and parked in front of a nail shop. The first thing that came to mind was he was there for a bitch. I parked some cars down, so I could see what he was doing. He sat in the car for about ten minutes before I saw the same big bitch come strutting out of the nail salon.

He got out the car and went to her. The two hugged and kissed, then started to have a conversation that had him smiling from ear to ear. I wish I could've heard what the fuck was so funny because he was just in a fucked-up ass mood. Shit just had me wondering what the fuck that bitch had on me. I looked better and I was pretty sure I fucked him better.

After conversing for a few minutes, he walked her to her car, then got in his. He fucked up when he decided to pull off before her. I used it as an opportunity to follow her; I had just hoped she wasn't going where he was. As soon as she pulled out, I drove right behind her. The best part about it was she didn't know my car, so she wouldn't had been alarmed if she saw it.

We drove about four blocks until Logan turned off, and she continued to go straight. I damn near jumped for joy because it was my chance to pull up on her ass. So many thoughts ran through my mind on what to do.

At first, I thought about waiting until she got to where she was going, get out and beat the dog shit out of her. But, then, I started to think; wait, that bitch was bigger than I was, by far. How would I look trying to be the bully and get my ass handed to me?

I knew I had to do something; I probably wouldn't have gotten the same opportunity again. The images of them being together plagued my mind, and I got mad and jealous all over again. My heart started to ache, knowing the man I loved was with someone else.

With no more care in the world, I mashed on the gas and slammed into the back of her car. But, instead of stopping, I kept my foot on the gas. She tried to drive off once she saw my face at an angle when the car twisted.

We both were flying down the expressway at full speed, but her little Honda wasn't a match for my Benz. I placed my car in sport mode and stomped on the gas again, catching up to her. Now, we were side by side and she looked me in the eye. She looked scared but didn't all the way panic.

I got something for that ass, I thought.

Allowing her to get ahead a bit, I lifted my foot off the gas for a moment, then stomped on it again. That time, I knew exactly what I wanted to do. I wanted to hit her so hard, her car flipped over, the way it did when she was in the Porsche.

I was feet away from her bumper when she swerved right, and I ended up tipping the side of her car. Instead of the other vehicle going off course, my car jumped in the air and flipped over and over again. I blacked out by the second flip.

CHAPTER 15

LOGAN

"Nigga, you funny as hell brah," I told Tione.

I was on the phone with that fool clowning for a quick minute. He'd been calling me every day since we reconnected, checking in and shit.

Beep!

I looked at my phone and saw Lyric was calling on the next line. "Aye, bro, it's my girl. Ima hit your line back."

"Aight, bet, lover boy," he laughed.

I clicked over to Lyric's call, and the first thing I heard was hysterical crying.

"Logan!" she howled.

"Lyric, what's wrong?" I asked in a panic.

"She tried to kill me, she tried to kill me, the babies, babies," she cried and kept repeating herself.

"Who? What? Where are you? Calm down and send ne your location right now," I told her.

I had literally just left her ass. She was at the nail salon getting pampered when I passed by and saw her for a hot second. I was about to make a move, so she went home and we said we'd link later that night.

"Okay, okay," she continued to cry.

Seconds later, a text message came through.

Queen: (Current Location)

"I'm only a few minutes away, stay on the phone," I told her.

She kept crying and talking about the babies. I was more than worried, but one thing that kind of kept me relaxed in a sense was she wasn't hurt badly where she couldn't talk.

I pressed so hard on my gas, dodging in and out of traffic, running stop signs and red lights to get to her. The GPS took me on the expressway and, when I looked, I was only about a minute away, that's when the traffic started to accumulate. I went onto the shoulder and drove pass everyone because in my mind, I knew all the hold-up had something to do with Lyric.

"You have reached your destination," Siri announced.

What I saw before my eyes was a wild ass scene. I saw Lyric's car banged up from behind and another car turned over. I jumped out my car and ran to Lyric's. When I got to her, she was covered in blood all over her face. I heard the sirens nearing, so I knew the police and ambulance was going to be arriving any minute, so I needed to know what the fuck happened.

"Baby, can you remember what happened?" I asked her.

"Your wife, she kept running into me; she was trying to run me off the road," she cried.

I turned and looked closely at the car that was flipped. I read the license plate, and it was Cat's. Immediately, my heart sank. While I was furious with what she tried to do, I didn't see her outside her vehicle, which only meant two things: she was dead or hurt really bad.

Before I could go over to see Cat's condition, the law reached, so I fell back and let them do their thing. I stayed by Lyric's side through everything. The ambulance wanted to take her, but I insisted on taking her to the hospital myself since she was awake and alert.

Once twelve gave me the green light to take her with their escort, I zoomed out of there with the quickness. Whoever the officer was that was driving ahead of us wasn't playing; he was making way for us and fast. Before I knew it, we were pulling up to the emergency room.

As I was getting out to get Lyric, a few doctors and nurses came out with a bed for her. The officer told me to leave my car, that it would be fine to go in with her.

They got Lyric out the car and onto the bed. I was following them in when I stopped for a second to ask the officer a question. "Hey, the other person in the other car, they okay?" I asked with concern.

Cat was on my shit list, but that didn't mean I wanted her to die. Honestly, I felt that was an easy way out of her pain; I needed her to live to feel it all.

"I'm not sure. I'll call over and find out for you," he stated.

"Appreciate it."

I turned and ran inside to see what was going on with Lyric. When I got back to her side, they were trying to get information on her, but she wasn't understanding them.

"Sir, is she allergic to anything, or is there any medical condition we should know about?" the doctor asked me.

"No, she's not allergic to anything and she's pregnant with twins. Please check on my babies and make sure all three of them are good," I spoke in a worried tone.

"Thanks for letting us know; we got it from here. Wait here while we work on her."

They pushed her through some doors and left me standing there not knowing what to do.

Just when I was about to let my thoughts get the best of me, a bunch of doctors and nurses came busting through the doors with someone on the bed. They were headed my way to go through the same doors Lyric went through. When they passed by, I saw it was Cat they were rushing inside. I was happy to see she was still alive, even if she was fighting; she had a chance.

I jumped on the phone and called Joe, my Uncle Frank and, then, I had to call Tione. Knowing Cat was in the hospital, I knew her father would drop what he was doing and hopped on his private jet. With that being said, I needed protection around, just in case shit went left when we ran into each other.

In the meantime, I went back outside and parked my car in a better spot. I knew the officer wasn't going to be able to save me from tickets or even being towed after a certain time as passed. After I moved my car, I hurried back inside to be on spot when they came out with any news or had any other questions.

Only twenty minutes had passed, and Joe and Uncle Frank came rushing into the ER. I clearly told them it wasn't me that was in the accident, but it just showed they cared about Lyric off the strength of me, and I appreciated that. Joe and Lyric had built a bond while we were all together for those few months, so I knew he would've been on go when it came to her. They sat by my side and didn't say a word; their presence was enough for me to feel the support.

An hour went by, and I still hadn't heard anything from the doctors, which made me antsy. I went up to the nurses' station to inquired about her condition but, of course, they had nothing for me. I tried my best to not worry because when I did part ways with her, she was still a little awake. I was more so concerned about the twins.

When I went back to sit down, I looked up and saw Tione and two of his boys walking in the sliding doors.

"Yo, bro!" he called out to me.

Joe and I both got up, leaving my uncle to sit back and watch.

"She cool?" he asked as he dapped me up.

"Last I seen her, she was. I just hope my seeds is good man," I blurted out.

That was the first time I actually told anyone besides Joe that Lyric was pregnant. It wasn't intentional; it just slipped out.

"What? Sis pregnant? Congratulations, don't worry, they going to pull through," he gave encouraging words.

"Good lookin' my boy."

While we were chopping it up, making small talk, I saw one of the doctors that rolled her in come out the double doors. We made eye contact, and he waved me over.

"Hold on, y'all," I told Tione and them as I jogged over to the doctor. "How is she? Are the babies fine?"

"Relax, she is doing just fine and the babies are good. She experience head trauma from the crash, had a gash on her head, some bruises on her face, and a concussion. Other than those things, she will be alright," he informed me.

I let out the deep breath I was holding the entire time he was speaking.

Thank you, Jesus, I praised Him.

"When will I be able to see her?"

"Ahhh, in a minute. They're actually transferring her from the emergency department room to a room upstairs. She has to stay a day or two for observation. The nurse can tell you the room they're taking her to."

"Thanks a lot, doc." I shook his hand. "Oh, one more thing. By chance, would you happen to know the condition of the other woman that was in the other car?"

"They're still working on her, that's all I can say."

"Okay, thanks man."

I went and told the guys the good news. My uncle told me he'd call me later; he just wanted to make sure everything was straight with her and to keep him posted on Cat's condition as well.

We waited a few before trying to head upstairs to where they took Lyric. Joe and Tione were plastered by my side while his boys were roaming around keeping their eyes and ears open for any Mexicans.

When we reached upstairs, the nurses directed us to Lyric's room without any problems. While I walked in, Joe and Tione stayed outside. Lyric seemed to be sleeping but, once I made it closer to her, I guess she felt my presence because her eyes popped open.

"Baby," she whined in a childlike tone.

Her head had a big bandage towards the front, her left eye was swollen black and blue, and her lips were busted. Even with all of that, I thought she was the most beautiful woman on planet earth.

"I'm here, baby girl. Shhh, get some rest," I told her.

I kissed her on her forehead and pulled up the covers higher over her chest. The lights were already dim in the room, which was a good thing. I didn't want anything to trigger any more pain to her concussion. As she drifted off to sleep, I sat beside her bed and held her hand while I rubbed her stomach with the other hand.

Damn near a whole day had passed, and we were still there. Tione and Joe hadn't moved; they were right inside the room with us. Lyric slept for hours, which was expected of her the doctors said. She needed all the rest she could to heal from the concussion.

"Man, y'all could go home and come back, ain't shit shaking," I told them.

"I'm good right here," Joe stated.

"Me too, brah," Tione added.

Just when Lyric started stir in her sleep, looking like she was about to wake up, a loud commotion erupted outside. Listening closely, it was a Spanish man. The moment we heard Spanish speaking, Joe and Tione jumped up from their seats and went outside. I stood up and pulled the blind all the way, so Lyric wasn't visible, not even a toe.

I walked to the door and saw it was Cat's father and uncle causing all the drama. Seeing them upstairs told me that Cat pulled through and was recovering. As he was walking past, he stopped when he saw me and gave me a menacing stare. His look didn't move me one bit. I stood there returning the same glare. I guess he was still pissed that I pulled a gun out on him and his daughter, but I didn't give a fuck. That short fuck didn't put no fear in my heart.

"And you wanted us to go home, right?" Tione looked at me and said with a knowing look.

I ducked back into the room to check on Lyric, and there she was lying there with her eyes opened.

"Sleeping beauty finally up," I joked. I bent down and pecked her bruised lips.

"How long was I out for?" she asked in a groggy voice.

"Oh, you sound bad baby," I cracked again.

She tried to hit me, but I backed away before she could reach me.

"Damn near a whole day, it's aight though. The doctors said you gotta sleep that concussion off."

She nodded her head up and down slow.

"Look, drink some of this water." I placed the straw to her lips, and she went ahead and drank some. "You hungry?"

"I'm starving," she replied.

"Aight, I'll have someone bring us something to eat. I know you ain't finna fuck with this hospital food." I raised the tray, uncovering the contents on the plate.

I called Tione in and told him to have one of his guys go grab some food for everyone. He ain't even asked a question; he just went ahead and pushed the order through.

We waited about an hour before he came with the grub. Everyone ate, including Lyric, and was full and satisfied. I just sat at her bedside and talked to her for the rest of the day.

"Oh baby, can I use your phone to call my sister?" she asked.

"Of course." I handed her my jack.

She dialed her up and waited for her to answer.

"Hey Lori, it's me, Lyric," she told her. "I had an accident and still in the hospital. Can you call Chadd and let him know that you're with me? I'll be home tomorrow, no need to come."

She was silent for a second. "Logan's with me, I'm fine," she informed her. "Okay, thanks. Love you, too."

"Where you trying to go, homie?" I heard Tione say.

"I want to see Logan," Cat's father requested.

"Hold on baby, I'll be right back," I told Lyric.

When I walked from behind the curtain, I saw him standing there with some of his guys. "What's the problem?" I asked as I moved towards him.

"We need to talk."

I nodded. "Tione, tell the guys I'm coming outside and stay with Lyric. Joe, let's go."

I walked out, and De Léon followed behind me. We got on the elevator and stayed quiet. It was that way until we reached outside. "Wassup?" I faced him.

"What happened to my daughter?" he came right out and asked.

"Your daughter tried to run my girlfriend off the road. Instead of my girl's car being trashed, Cat ended up fuckin' herself up," I explained to him.

He stayed quiet for a minute. "So, you and her are over with?" he went on and asked.

"Yes, I filed for a divorce. Your daughter has betrayed me not once but twice. It's no going back."

"And your father?"

"I will deal with him accordingly. There's something coming his way soon."

"Logan, your father made a bad move when he decided to deal with my daughter behind your back. He allowed Catteleya to disgrace herself; it's no forgiving there."

"I understand, trust me, I agree. So, I take it as no business has been going on since then."

"No, no more business. If you want business with me, he has to go."

I knew my father, and him not making any moves together put a big dent in everyone's pockets, from my father straight down to the maid. It wasn't just about money and power; it was about providing for the families that been there for us.

"What if I can get him out of here? Will you resume business and forget I pulled a gun on you?" I watched him closely.

"Sí, I will."

"We have a deal, but I might need you to do something for me," I told him.

"Just let me know."

We shook hands, and I felt the tension between us dissolve. In the end, we both wanted the same thing in a way; my father to be dethroned and gone. Now, it was time to put a plan together.

KAYLA

It was only a matter of time either Chadd or Kevin was going to ask me for a DNA test. I just didn't expect it to be Kevin asking for one while I was still carrying. He made it a point to stress the fact that he didn't want to wait the full nine months not knowing if it was his or not, that it would be unfair to him and Chadd.

After he kept singing the song in my head, I went ahead and scheduled an appointment to get the test done. When I said it was uncomfortable, that was an understatement. Overall, I was happy it got done and all I had to do was wait for the results. I only had the baby's sample tested against Kevin's. I didn't tell Chadd about the uncertainty I had about who the father was; plus, he still didn't know who Kevin was.

One morning, I woke up and started getting ready for work. Kevin wasn't in bed with me, so I looked all around the apartment. He'd been staying out and doing whatever it was he caught himself doing, but I didn't stress myself about it. I prayed so badly that it wasn't his, so I'd been able to get away from his foolishness.

By the time I got out the shower, I heard the front door open and shut. I continued to get ready for work and didn't pay him no mind with all the noise he was making in the kitchen. While I was applying my make-up, my phone vibrated and it was a message from Chadd.

> Chadd: Please make sure you're on time, we have to prep for the closing on the new account.

As I was reading the message, I felt someone staring at me. I looked up and saw it was Kevin, standing in the doorway glaring at me.

"Didn't I tell you to quit your job?" he slurred.

By the way he spoke, I knew he was high and drunk.

"I have to find another job before I can quit, Kevin," I simply told him. I didn't want to argue or say anything to trigger him.

He started to laugh an almost evil laugh and just walked away.

Should I be worried? I asked myself.

Trying to get away from him fast as possible, I hurriedly finished getting myself together and jetted out the apartment before we could get into it.

When I got in my car and was getting ready to pull off, I received a text from Kevin.

> Kev: I see you just don't listen, but don't worry, you'll learn your lesson.

I hated when he spoke in codes to deliver a threat, and I wouldn't be lying if I said I wasn't scared.

There was nothing I could do in that moment, so I just continued on my way to work, hoping for a good day. It was becoming tough to deal with Kevin's insecurities and Chadd's ignorant ways all at once. I was just one person, and I was at a point where I couldn't take things no more.

When I arrived at work, Chadd was already there and in tune with his workload. I saw a pile of things on my desk that I had to attack, so I didn't even waste my time saying hi to him. Our days became like that, barely speaking a word to one another unless we absolutely had to.

I sat at my desk and jumped right into what was in front of me before I had to meet with him about the account closing. Halfway into the morning, one of the big bosses of the firm, Steven, came and asked to speak to me. As I got up and walked away, I saw Chadd looking at me with a concerned look. I had a mind this random meeting was pertaining to the audit they were conducting on Chadd.

When I walked into the conference room, there were two other owners already seated. I didn't know why I thought it was just a one-on-one thing with Steven and I, so I wasn't nervous, but seeing all three of them made me want to shit my pants.

"Ms. Bridges, how are you today?" one of the guys asked.

"I'm fine, thanks for asking. How are you all?" I retorted.

"Good," they all said in a unison like it was planned.

"We wanted to speak to you about Mr. Larson and how he handles his accounts," Steven spoke up and said.

"Okay, what about it?" I quizzed.

"Do he follow all policies when it comes to opening and handling the accounts under him?"

"That I know of, yes."

"Do he have any close relationships with any of his clients, like outside of doing business?"

"No, not that I know of." I had to be very careful how I answered to not incriminate Chadd or myself.

"Do you know if Chadd himself opened an account under himself and did not notify the company about doing so?"

"No, I'm unaware of anything like that."

"Ms. Bridges, please know that if we find out you knew anything other than you're saying, you—"

"Where the fuck that clear nigga Chadd at?" I heard a familiar voice yell, cutting of Steven's statement.

We all stood up from our seats to see what was going on. Leaving the conference room, I saw it was Kevin making all that noise.

"Oh, fuck no," I whispered, covering my mouth in disbelief.

"Sir, calm down. What's all this about?" one of the owners stepped up and asked Kevin.

"Aye, my man, back the fuck up. I just want to holler at Chadd; I think his last name Lanson or Larson, some shit like that. Matter of fact, where's that bitch Kayla Bridges? She know why I'm here."

Everyone immediately turned in my direction, and I felt so embarrassed. Chadd came walking out his office and down the hall towards us. I wanted to push him back so badly, but I already knew he wanted to know what the hell was going on and why was some strange man calling out his name like they knew each other.

"What's all this about, who are you?" Chadd asked as he reached the scene.

At this time, security was called and they had arrived.

"You been fucking my girlfriend, Kayla. Now, she's pregnant and don't know if the baby mine and yours." He pointed at Chadd in a playful manner.

Everyone's eyes bounced back and forth between Chadd and me. I lowered my head because I just couldn't believe that shit was happening.

"Wait, you've been having an affair with your assistant?" Steven intervened.

We stayed silent, but Kevin spoke up for the both of us.

"Yup, and he been giving her loads of money for the pussy," he added.

Then and there, I just wanted to cry and disappear.

"Sir, please come with us," one of the security officers told Kevin.

"Bro, do not touch me. I will wild this place up."

No, please don't, I said in my head.

"Fine but you have to leave. We're giving you the option to walk out on your own but, if you don't comply, we will have no other choice but to remove you," they told him.

Kevin didn't take threats too kindly so, of course, he showed his ass. "I'm not going nowhere and, the moment you touch me, it's on."

Everyone's face was shocked while some people looked a bit nervous. The officers grabbed Kevin by both his arms and another officer held his feet. They literally carried him off the floor and out the building in that manner.

Everything got quiet, but the stares were loud as fuck. I slowly walked back to my desk and just placed my head on it.

"You had a boyfriend all this time?" Chadd came and asked.

I raised my head and just looked at him. "You had a wife all this time?" I retorted.

Before neither of us could get another word out, Steven walked up on us.

"I think it's best you two go home for the remainder of the day," he advised.

"But I have an account to close, Steven."

"Go home," he stated again and walked away.

"This is on you," Chadd said and pointed at me.

We both got our things together and left the office. While it wasn't planned, we ended up on the elevator together while going down to the parking garage.

When we got off, we started to walk our separate ways until Kevin jumped out of nowhere, pointing a gun at us.

"You think your white privileged ass was going to get away? They saved you for the time being, but I knew I was gon' catch up with you," he spat.

I could told he was still under the influence.

"Kevin, please, don't do this," I plead to him.

"Bitch, shut yo nasty, hoe ass up," he snapped and aimed the gun at me.

"I don't know who you are. Kayla never told me she had a boyfriend, or else I wouldn't have even got involved with her," Chadd explained.

"But don't you have a wife, muthafucker? You shouldn't have gotten involved in the first place."

"That's true, and I'm paying for that now. We can come to some sort of understanding and conclusion."

"Yeah, you're right. I came up with the best solution," Kevin exclaimed.

"And what's that?" Chadd asked.

Kevin pulled the trigger twice, shooting Chadd in the neck and chest. Once he dropped to the ground, he let off another three shots before he ran off.

"Nooo!" I screamed. "No, no, no." I dropped down and tried to apply pressure to his wounds, but there were too many.

"Please, somebody help!" I yelled out as I pressed down on his neck.

Chadd was fighting, but I knew it was only a matter of time before the darkness took him. He started to choke on his own blood uncontrollably. I tried my best to keep him still and do everything I was taught in the hood to do when someone got shot, but it didn't seem to work.

Tears fell down my face as I held him in my arms. I felt his soul leave his body and, when he stopped choking or moving, I knew that was it. I closed his eyes and just sat there and waited for someone to find us.

My phone chimed with an email alert on the ground next to us. The preview said it was from the medical lab with the test results. Something told me to click it, so I did.

The baby was Kevin's.

CHAPTER 17

LYRIC

Experiencing yet another life-threatening event had spooked me and had me in a real bad mental head space. I was grateful I walked away with just some bruises and a concussion. I was told Catteleya was broke up in all different places and had a lot of internal bleeding. I didn't wish death upon anyone, not even my worst enemy but, if she didn't pull through, I wouldn't have batted an eye or cared.

Surprisingly, Chadd didn't push to come to the hospital. He was really giving me my space and listened to what I wanted, so I was grateful for that. I didn't know how I'd handle both Logan and him running into each other. It just wasn't the right time for things to come out yet. Plus, I wanted Logan by my side; he was my peace and, although he felt he was to blame for what happened, I didn't think so.

I was discharged two days after the accident once they saw all my test results were good and that I seemed to had been progressing in that short period of time. The babies were fine and that was my main concern, so home it was for me to heal.

The same day I was discharged, my lawyer called me and asked that I come into her office immediately to sign something. It was urgent, and she needed to file something with the court within that same day. I told Logan what I had going on, so he said he'd go with me, then take me home afterwards. I was grateful Logan had Joe run and pick me up some clothes to leave with, making it easy to just go deal with Mrs. Daniels right away instead of going home first to change.

"You sure you good to go in alone?" Lo asked me.

"Yeah, I'm fine, baby," I assured him.

We had pulled up to Mrs. Daniels' office, and I wanted to run in and out. The main thing on my mind was getting home to my bed. My body was aching badly and was calling for a hot bath and some rest.

"Aight, I'll be right here waiting."

I nodded and slowly exited the car. When I made it inside, the receptionist told me to go right into the office, which was open. I knocked lightly as I poked my head inside to see if she was indeed free.

"Lyric, hey, come in," she greeted me once she saw me in the doorway. "Whoa, what happened to you?" she asked once I got closer and she saw the condition of my face.

"I was in a car accident, I just got discharged," I answered.

"If I had known, I would've came to you. Oh my, are you okay?"

"Yeah, I'm alive, so I can't complain."

"Here, I need you to sign this last piece of paper for me, I need to expedite the filings."

"Okay, cool." I signed where she marked and that was it.

"I'll keep you updated along the way."

"Thank you."

When I walked out the building, I saw Lo standing outside his car with a weird look on his face.

"What's wrong?" I asked.

"Your sister called, she said to call her back now; it's urgent."

I was wondering how she had gotten Lo's number and why she just didn't call me. That's when I remembered that after the accident, I lost my phone and used Lo's to call her. Lo made sure and got me a replacement phone, which Lori-Ann and I spoke about before, but I left it in the car when I went in to see Mrs. Daniels.

When I got in the car, I called her right way.

"Lyric?" she answered on the first ring.

"Yeah, everything okay?"

"No, get home, now!" she raised her voice but it was shaky.

"Okay, I'll be right there."

"Bae, get me home, please. Something's up," I told him.

"Aight."

Not wasting another second, Lo placed the car in drive and pressed on gas straight to my house.

About twenty minutes later, we turned on my block but, from a distance, I was able to see some commotion going on in what I assumed to be my house. The first thing I thought was my shit was on fire or something but, as I got closer, the house looked fine.

There were two police patrol cars out front, along with an unmarked car that detectives rode in. The officers were all out their cars and waiting around. I spotted Lori-Ann in the driveway with Nick.

What the hell is going on? I thought.

Logan pulled up directly in front the house, and I jumped out right away. Lori and Nick rushed up to me with two detectives behind them.

"What's going on? Why are all these cops at my house?" I asked them.

"Lyric, I'm sorry," Lori-Ann said with tears in her eyes.

"What is it?"

"Chadd was murdered today," she blurted out.

I felt myself get lightheaded and, before I knew it, my knees gave out on me.

"Tell them they have to wait. She's clearly recovering from an accident, then have to deal with this shit," I heard Nick say in a hushed tone.

I opened my eyes to see I was lying in my bed. The last I remembered was being out front of my house hearing some crazy ass news from Lori-Ann. I knew I had to be dreaming.

"What y'all talking about?" I asked, scaring them.

"Hey, love, how are you feeling?" Nick asked as he came to my bedside.

"I'm okay, my head is pounding but I'm cool."

"We'll get you something for that," Lori stated.

"Why did I have a crazy dream y'all said Chadd was murdered?" I giggled.

Nick and Lori looked at each other with regretful looks.

"Baby, because you weren't dreaming, it's true," Nick exclaimed.

Tears welled in my eyes because I just didn't know why so many bad things were happening to me. Most people would've been happy to receive that kind of news after all he had done but not me. I still had a heart and, although he played a part in crushing it, he also was a part of many special moments in my life that I couldn't erase.

"How?" I asked above a whisper.

"Kayla's boyfriend went to their job, confronted him about their affair, and shot him multiple times," Nick explained.

I held my hands over my nose and mouth. It became hard for me to breathe.

"Relax, Lyric, take deep breaths," Nick coached. "Go get her some water."

I did what he said and took deep breaths, inhaling and exhaling. Lori-Ann returned with water and some Tylenol for me to take. I popped the pill and gulped down the glass of water.

"The detectives gave us their card for you. They wanted to talk, but I told them not right now. Besides, it's nothing they need from you; they know who killed him and why," Nicked remarked.

"Yeah, I'm really not up for talking to anyone honestly. Please, can y'all handle everything for me? Don't leave," I begged them both.

"Nah uh girl, we're here, don't even worry," Nick assured me.

"Where's Logan?" I finally realized he was the one who brought me home.

"Oh, that man is still outside in his car. Haven't moved yet."

"What?"

"Yup, he said he'll stay out there until you woke up and he knew you was fine. He mentioned something about respecting another man's house, a dead one at that," Lori stated.

"Call him for me, please."

She pulled her phone from her back pocket and handed it to me with his number on the screen. I pressed call and let it ring.

"Hello?" he answered.

"Logan," I spoke into the phone.

"I don't even want to ask you are you okay. I know you fucked up right now," he assumed. "I'll give you your space until you're ready. Just know I'm here."

"Okay," I said softly.

"I love you," he voiced.

"I love you, too."

The phone went dead, and I handed it back to Lori. I pulled the blanket over me, closed my eyes, and forced myself to go back to sleep, hoping it was all a dream.

CHAPTER 13

LOGAN

If it wasn't one thing, it was the next. Hella shit had been happening around both Lyric and me, and a nigga just couldn't take it anymore. From the minute my father gave me the assignment to get close to her, my life hadn't been the same; it had been in a constant uproar. Betrayals, accidents, shootings, and deaths just took over our lives. It was like there was a dark cloud hanging over us.

When I found out about Chadd, I was in straight disbelief; I knew they had to be bullshitting. Him being murdered the way he did just wasn't something I pictured. I knew I had plans to take him out, even though Lyric said it wasn't no need to, but I took it as the job was done for me.

Lyric was already in the process of filing for a divorce, unbeknownst to him, and was prepared to fight and drain him of everything he had. God always worked in mysterious ways. There was no fight for Lyric to have; He made sure of that. As his widow with no children, every single penny, drawers he owned, and dust in his pants pocket was now Lyric's.

I gave her some space when everything went down. I knew it was tough on her; plus, she was still recovering from her accident. Lyric was one strong ass woman because she done endured so much in a short period of time that most women would've already folded and tapped out.

When I arrived home to my condo after leaving Lyric's place, I got a phone call from my Pops. I contemplated on if to answer or not because I knew he was calling due to everything that had been going on, from Cat and Lyric's accident to possibly even Chadd's death. My father was well connected and had eyes and ears everywhere.

"Hello?" I decided to pick up the call.

"Congratulations, Son, you won the girl indefinitely," he almost gloated on my behalf.

"Pa, really? Too soon, man."

"What? Weren't you—" he stopped in his tracks, "never mind."

"I want to celebrate everyone getting what they want. Dinner at my house tomorrow for seven, and I'm not taking no for an answer."

I pinched the bridge of my nose because who told me to

answer this man's call? "Okay, Pa. I'll see you tomorrow," I gave in.

"Great, see you tomorrow. Don't be late," he said before hanging up.

I laid across the foot of my bed while looking up at the ceiling. My mind went on Lyric and how she was feeling; then, it shifted to how Cat was making out in her recovery; then, it went to my father and how I could get him out of the picture.

Although he called a truce, I knew him too well. He felt a certain way about me pulling a gun out on him, any real man would. He also did some unthinkable things that I could've never forgave him for. He didn't just fuck my wife; he was fucking my wife, then had the nerve to try to have me killed. He also put the love of my life and our children in harm's way. His time was coming and, the way everything was happening, I knew it was going to be soon.

I laid there just thinking and thinking, and something hit me. Jumping up, I went looking for my phone. When I located it, I called both Joe and Tione and told them to meet me at my spot. While I waited for their arrival, I grabbed myself something to eat and studied my father's layout of his home.

Joe arrived first, of course, because he was the closest, but Tione never let up on the gas so he was on the island and at my crib in under an hour.

"I think it's time shit get a little nasty. I'm ready to put some things to rest, so I can move on with my life," I announced to both gentlemen.

"About time," Joe exclaimed.

It was like he knew what I was thinking. "Tomorrow, we take my father out, but I know the person who will actually pull the trigger."

"Who?" Joe asked.

"De Léon."

The following day, I woke up feeling like the day was going to be a great one. I loved the feeling of being free and not having enemies right under my nose in my camp, especially when the person was my own flesh and blood.

After Joe, Tione, and I met, we came up with a solid plan which included getting an army involved. I made my call to De Léon, who was still on the island due to Cat's condition. Without saying but so many words, he understood and was more than happy to join us for dinner.

I told her what needed to be told and kept the circle small. Uncle Frank was going to be in attendance at the dinner, but I felt it wasn't right to include him. I didn't want to put him in a fucked-up predicament where he felt he needed to choose.

For the entire day, I stayed inside. I shot Lyric a few texts, checking in on her, and just stayed in my head the rest of the day. I replayed the plan over and over to myself, making sure there wasn't anything I was missing. I probably went over it a million times, no joke. I wasn't a perfectionist; I just didn't play when it came to my life.

The day went by fast as hell and, before I knew it, it was

time for me to get ready and head over to my father's estates. I checked in with everybody to make sure they were on point, and they were. Joe was in charge of things since I had to go inside first.

I got dressed in some designer as usual, looking and feeling good. Making things look and feel normal was the key for the night. On my way out, I shot Lyric a text message.

> Me: I hope my baby girl is taking it easy over there with my babies. Know that I love y'all and daddy will see y'all soon.

I didn't expect her to text me right back due to her being busy with people and doing funeral arrangements and shit.

Checking my guns, they were all loaded and ready to fire. I cranked up my engine and pulled out of my complex and headed to my destination. Of course, it didn't take me a long time to reach his house; we didn't live far from one another. As I was driving through the gate, my phone chimed, indicating I received a text.

> Queen: And we love you more daddy, see you soon. Be good. (Heart emoji).

I pulled up to the front and saw there were a good number of cars outside that weren't my father's. When he did dinners, he usually invited all the bosses that sat at the table under him, which included my Uncle Frank. It was a perfect night to set the record straight; everyone was going to be in attendance.

Making my way inside, I bypassed Phil at the door and headed for the dining room where I saw most people were already seated.

"There he go," my father announced when I walked in.

"Good evening, everyone," I greeted the room.

All the men spoke back and nodded their head. My father motioned for me to take a seat at the opposite head of the table, so I did just that. Everyone was already having some sort of conversation with one another. I just sat there and observed everyone and the whole scenery. I texted Joe and Tione to let them know I was in and, so far, so good. After quickly skimming the premises when I came in, I informed of the number of guards that were visible and where they were.

While I fed them intel, it was up to them and De Léon to properly infiltrate and make their way inside the house. We had two armies: Tione's, and De Léon's. With the large amount, I knew for a fact we outnumbered my father's guys.

I got a text from Joe stating they were in position and was waiting for the green light from me. Just when I read his message, the chef and his crew came out with the first set of dishes. I thought why not allow him to enjoy his last set of meals; it was only right. Dish after dish came out, and I couldn't lie; they all tasted good as fuck. All that brainstorming ran a nigga's appetite up, so I gladly enjoyed the food.

The entire time, my father barely spoke to me. He kept on with his conversation with his pairs, which was cool with me;

we ain't have shit to talk about. I did catch him looking at me off and on though, on some weird shit.

Feeling like it was time to get shit going, I shot Joe the text and told him it's go time. I just sat back and waited. The gentlemen were eating their desserts and discussing business matters when a De Léon walked in and stood behind me. The look on my father's face was priceless, because there was not one sound of a gunshot that went off. I specifically told them to make things quiet, so they used my favorite tool, a silencer to clear out the premises. And judging by the fact Joe, Tione, De Léon, and their guys were inside the house, it told me they understood the assignment.

"What the hell is going on?" My father jumped up from his seat.

Everyone around the table was confused about what was going on, including my uncle.

"You thought you could fuck my daughter's life up and get away with it?" De Léon asked as he walked closer to my father.

I sat quiet in my seat and enjoyed the show; there was nothing for me to say or do.

"Who knew about this?" my father asked, looking around the room.

All men gave him a shrug because they were clueless. He looked straight at me with a hateful glare. If looks could kill, I would've been dead where I sat.

"You son of a bitch," he spat my way.

"De Léon, please," I turned and told him.

He raised his gun and emptied his whole clip in my father,

as everyone looked on. Not a soul moved to defend him, not even my uncle. My father turned into the very man he hated: his father, my grandfather. Everyone was tired and fed up with how he ran things and, obviously, he couldn't do things right since he fucked up the money flow. It was time for change, and I made the move to make it happen.

When one man went down, his son took his place. That's how the mob worked, but I didn't want the position; I had someone else in mind that was perfect.

"I know I assume the title and responsibility as the head of the organization now, but it won't be me. I acknowledge Frank Luchiano will be your leader," I announced.

Everyone around the table gasped and clapped their hands. From what I was able to tell, I made the perfect choice, and they agreed.

I could have carried on the family legacy myself, but I knew it would've been a tough road as a black man being the head of an Italian mafia. Although it was my birthright, it was also my uncle's.

"Party is over, y'all can leave." I waved them off.

Uncle Frank made his way over to me with the quickness. He extended his hand, as I did the same.

"Thank you, kid." He smiled.

"It's only right."

De Léon approached us and, while I thought my uncle would've been a little off, he was accepting of him.

"De Léon will be back in business with us now that my father is out the way. You now have the full responsibility of everything. As for me, I'll always be a Luchiano, but I'm building my own organization, one that will be strong, loyal, and about their money. It'll be something like a black mafia and I'm their Don." I looked at Joe and Tione.

I shook both my uncle and De Léon's hands.

"Let's do business fellas."

EPILOGUE

LYRIC

About five months later...

"Push, push," the doctor instructed.

"Come on, baby, push," Logan coached me, as I squeezed his hands.

They kept yelling in my ear to push as if I wasn't fuckin' pushing. Listen, having a baby ain't no joke, so imagine trying to push out two.

"I'm pushinggg, God damnit," I snapped.

"Alright, I see the head, there we go," Doctor Rice exclaimed.

Hearing one of the babies was right there gave me all the motivation I needed to just push hard despite the pain. "Ugghhhrrr!" I roared.

"Yayyy!" I heard everyone in the room erupt in celebration.

I looked down and saw baby number one was out.

"Congratulations, it's a boy," they announced.

Logan and I agreed on not finding out the genders; we wanted it to be a surprise. So, I knew he was ecstatic that he got his boy that he was claiming from the moment we found out I was pregnant.

"I feel the other one coming down!" I yelled.

"Alright, give me another big push," Doc said.

I used all the might I had and pushed really hard.

"Yes, the head, we got the head."

I took some deep breaths in and out before I got ready for another push.

"You ready?" Doctor Rice asked.

I looked up at Logan, who was smiling hard as shit.

"Yeah."

"Push, Lyric, push!"

"Ughhh," I moaned out.

"She's out!" Doctor Rice announced. "Congratulations, it's a girl."

I couldn't have been happier. God blessed me with my boy and girl in one shot. He knew there would've been a chance I couldn't get pregnant again, so he delivered the most precious gifts to Logan and me.

"I love you, baby, thank you so much," Logan exclaimed as he rocked our baby boy side to side in his arms.

The nurse brought our little girl over to me. I cried tears of joy to see two humans who grew inside of me make it out safely into the world. It was a blissful feeling; it was priceless.

Life threw so many curveballs my way, but I dodged each and every one of them. I was heartbroken, kidnapped, been in life-ending accidents, lost a husband but gained the love of my life all in under a year.

I had no clue my life would've turned out the way it did. It wasn't perfect, but everyone in it was perfect to me. I grew in so many ways that I didn't even know was possible. I learned to love unconditionally, and I learned to accept being loved the right way.

I couldn't believe I could say, "Thank God, I was Snatched Up by a Don."

Acknowledgments

Whew! This series was one hell of a ride, but I truly enjoyed it. I hope you all loved it as much as I loved writing it. Thank you so much for supporting me yet again. Without you, there's no me!

-P. Wise

About the Author

P. Wise (Pretti Wise) is a National and International Best Selling author of fiction literature, whose experiences and imagination have shaped her to write about her ideas. She is originally from

Trinidad and Tobago but grew up in Bed-Stuy, Brooklyn; also spent a great deal of time in Philadelphia and Chester.

Having experienced and witnessed different events in her life, she has a variety of perspectives that almost any and everyone can understand. The love to write stemmed from a young age, as she enjoyed essay writing and penning her journal.

Coming from a lower-class family, she's a first-generation college graduate, but also, the first to enter and survive a federal prison sentence. With ambition, intelligence, and absurdly high tenacity, she'll have her place in the fiction game.

P. Wise has a 2 year old daughter, who's her world and reason for her grind.

This is P.Wise's Thirteenth book since starting her career in January 2022.

Stay Connected!

Website: PrettiWise.com

   Instagram: @CEO.Pwise

   Facebook: Author P. Wise

   Facebook Business: Authoress P. Wise

   Facebook Group: Words of the Wise (P. Wise Book Group)

Also by P. Wise

Made in United States
North Haven, CT
28 July 2023

39647937R00104